Fourth of July
Lewis J. Beilman III
Scarlet Leaf
2017

PUBLISHED BY SCARLET LEAF

Toronto, Canada

Fourth of July

Ogden stood at the threshold. He was a handsome, middle-aged man, about six-feet tall, with broad shoulders, hazel eyes, and sandy hair. With a starched white handkerchief, he dabbed the sweat that had collected on his forehead after his walk home from the office. He returned the handkerchief to his breast pocket, brushed off the lapels of his navy-blue sports coat, and took his keys from his pant pocket. It was a late Friday evening in June, and he was returning from the commercial-acquisitions firm at which he was a senior partner.

Ogden opened the door.

The light from the setting sun shone through a large window that overlooked the east side of Central Park. The sunlight illuminated the profiles of his wife and son, who sat on a black leather sofa in the center of the television room. Charles, the family's Boston Terrier, nestled in between them. The mother and son watched a program on the television but turned to greet Ogden as he walked in. His son jumped from the sofa and raced across the wooden floor, sliding over the slick surface in his socks. Ogden scooped him up, tossing him in the air before catching him in open arms.

"Daddy, I'm so glad you're home," his son said.

"I couldn't wait to see you either, Johnny," Ogden said. As he held the boy, Charles danced around Ogden's feet.

Ogden's wife, Sarah, followed close behind her son, straightening the skirt of her dress as she approached. Ogden returned Johnny to the floor. Sarah's blue eyes and the diamond studs in her ears sparkled beneath the recessed lighting of the entryway. She smiled as Ogden embraced her. He brushed her blonde hair from her cheek and kissed her. "This makes the rest of the day worthwhile," he said, squeezing her close to him. He smelled the fragrance of lily-of-the-valley on her nape, and the scent reminded him of long-ago summers spent vacationing at his family's cottage upstate.

"I'm glad you're home early tonight," Sarah said. "Maria's just about to set the table."

In the background, their housekeeper shuffled from the kitchen to the dining area. She wore a black dress and white apron and had her hands full with plates and silverware. The lower level of the two-story condominium had a stark open design with white unadorned walls. The floor plan allowed easy access from one area to the next, and the family—Charles in tow—walked together to the table. They sat down, Ogden at the head of the table and Sarah and Johnny on either side of him.

Maria carried a covered sterling-silver tray to the table. She set it down between a Waterford serving bowl filled with mashed potatoes and another filled with corn. "It's Friday," Maria said, lifting the dome from the silver tray. "I made your favorite, Mr. Goodman." Although Maria had lived in the city most of her life, her voice still carried a slight Puerto Rican accent.

"Ham and mashed potatoes," Ogden said, clapping his hands. "Once again, you've outdone yourself, Maria. May I do the honors?" He stood and reached for the carving knife.

"Certainly, Mr. Goodman," Maria said. As he carved the ham, she poured wine from a crystal decanter for Sarah and water from a glass pitcher for Ogden, Johnny, and her. She then placed servings of the side dishes on each plate. When she had finished, she sat at Johnny's right. Ogden placed a slice of ham on each person's plate and dropped a shaving on the floor for Charles.

"Let's say a few words of thanks before we start," Ogden said, sitting down again. They held one another's hands and bowed their heads. "Dear God, thank you for providing this bounty to us. We are humbled by your generosity. Amen."

"Amen," said Sarah, Johnny, and Maria in unison.

"Now let's eat," Ogden said.

They dug in.

AFTER HAVING FINISHED dinner, the family bade Maria farewell. She gathered her purse, hugged Johnny goodbye, and departed for the weekend. The family moved to the sofa, where they stared at a broad flat-screen television affixed to an otherwise bare wall. The television dominated the room. Ogden held the remote control in his right hand and searched for a program that he and his family could enjoy. His left arm draped across Sarah's shoulders, and Charles lay across his lap. Johnny, in khaki shorts and a blue short-sleeve dress shirt, sat on Ogden's other side. Brightly colored images flitted before their eyes: a yellow-and-white cheetah with black spots pursued a tawny antelope; two redheaded hillbillies in blue overalls chased a pair of pink pigs through a mucky pen; and a bronze-skinned Latina in a shimmering red-sequined dress belted out The Rhythm Is Gonna Get You.

And so on.

Ogden spoke at a clip with each press of a button: "Boring—Seen it—This again?"

"There's nothing on," Johnny whined. "Why?"

"I wish I could tell you," Ogden said, tousling his son's hair. "It's hard to fathom. We have a thousand channels and not a single thing to watch." He clenched his teeth.

"Oh, honey," Sarah said. "Don't get upset." She patted Ogden's leg softly.

"Forgive me, darling, but I'm furious," Ogden said, shaking his head. He took Charles in his hands and stood up. "I can bear this nonsense no longer. I'm taking little Charlie here for a walk. Would it please you to join me, Johnny?"

"Sure, Daddy," Johnny said. "I don't want to watch this stupid TV anymore." He squeezed his fists at his side.

"Well, grab Charlie's leash then," Ogden said. "Sarah, would you like to come along?"

"No, honey," she said. She grabbed the remote control from where Ogden had been sitting. "I'll wait here. I'm sure if I keep trying I'll find something worth watching."

"Suit yourself, darling," Ogden said. He bent from his waist, kissed Sarah on the forehead, and set Charles on the floor. "We'll be back soon enough."

FATHER AND SON WALKED along a dark-cement path in the park. Runners, fellow dog-walkers, and a variety of bums passed them in either direction. Undistracted, Charles sniffed about the path's grassy border, occasionally lifting a black-and-white leg to spritz the uncut dandelions and buttercups. After they had walked a quarter mile or so into the park, Charles hunched over, looked from side-to-side, and defecated. Ogden, leash in hand, clapped briefly. "Huzzah!" he said. "Good boy, Charlie." He took a small plastic bag from his pocket, crouched, and retrieved Charles' feces.

"Look, Daddy," Johnny said, pointing to a used condom. "Charlie pooped by a balloon."

Ogden shook his head in disgust. "Johnny," he said. "I'll never understand how people can sully our precious park without a pang of conscience." He stared at the golden sperm-filled receptacle, which lay within five feet of a garbage can. "I hope you never think of throwing your trash willy-nilly in a public space." He walked to the condom, picked it up with his plastic bag, and disposed of the feces and seed in the garbage can. He wiped his hands together and sighed. "Let that be a lesson in citizenship to you, young man" he said, wagging his finger at Johnny. "Now, let's go home."

As they walked back toward their building, a panhandler approached them. He wore ragged dungarees and a begrimed gray T-shirt. His scraggly red hair and beard obscured his weathered face. He looked fifty, but could have been thirty-five. "Could you spare some change, mister?" he said.

"Certainly," Ogden said, looking the panhandler in the eye. The panhandler averted his gaze. Johnny, his head at Ogden's waist, clutched his father's leg. Ogden reached into his pant pocket, fished out two quarters, and handed them to the man. The man nodded, mumbled a few words of thanks, and walked away.

"Why did that man ask you for money?" Johnny said, still gripping Ogden's leg. His pale eyes looked up inquiringly from beneath his mop of white hair.

"You'll understand someday that some people aren't as fortunate as we are," Ogden said. He patted the boy on his head—but he realized he didn't truly know the answer to Johnny's question. Was the panhandler sick, lazy, or just unlucky? he thought. Pondering the panhandler's situation, he stood still for a moment before he came to an abrupt conclusion. Wouldn't it be better for his family to learn the panhandler's plight than to spend another evening watching a harebrained movie, nonsensical reality show, or vapid infomercial? He looked over his shoulder, saw the panhandler was only a short distance away, and handed Charles' leash to Johnny.

Johnny screwed up his eyes. "Where are you going, Daddy?" he said.

"Wait one minute, son," Ogden said, taking off in pursuit of the panhandler. "I'll be right back."

WHEN OGDEN REACHED the panhandler, he squared his shoulders, raised his dimpled chin, and spoke with measured assurance. "Listen, my good man," he said. "How would you like to earn two-hundred dollars for two hours of work?" He folded his arms in front of his chest. He felt most at ease in life when he was negotiating a deal.

The man looked askance at Ogden and stepped backward. His voice croaked, presumably from years of hard living. "I don't do anything kinky," he said, nodding in the direction of Johnny. "Especially not with kids."

"Good sir, I take offense at that insinuation," Ogden said. "I merely want to educate my family on the travails of the common man. If you do not wish to assist me in this process of edification, I can most assuredly find someone else who will be more than willing to help."

"OK," the panhandler said, stepping closer to Ogden. "I'll do it—but for two-fifty."

"You drive a hard bargain," Ogden said. "Two-twenty-five—and that's my final offer."

The panhandler rubbed his beard, looked side to side, and reached his conclusion. "Deal," he said, holding his hand out to Ogden. Ogden shook the man's dusty hand.

OGDEN AND THE PANHANDLER joined Johnny, and the three of them walked with Charles toward the condominium. Ogden walked in the center, with Johnny to his right. "Johnny," Ogden said, "when we get home, this man will answer any question you might have." Ogden looked at the panhandler. "Right, my friend?"

"Yes, sir," the panhandler said. Out of the blue, he goose-stepped and saluted the emptiness in front of them. "I'll tell your son all he wants to know about my illustrious life."

Johnny stood close to his father and clutched tightly on Charles' leash. He stared at his feet while he walked. Under his breath, he hummed "When Johnny Comes Marching Home," the first song his father had taught him. He sang softly at the lines, "And we'll all feel gay / when Johnny comes marching home."

"That-a-boy, Johnny!" Ogden said. "You know I love that song."

When they reached the entrance to the building, the doorman, looking slightly concerned, approached Ogden. "Mr. Goodman, is everything all right this evening?"

Ogden put his hand on the doorman's shoulder. "Everything is quite all right, Billy," he said. He signaled to Johnny and the panhandler to wait where they were, and he and the doorman walked from beneath the scarlet awning that covered the entryway. Ogden continued their conversation on the sidewalk in some semblance of privacy. "I know the man accompanying me may not appear to be of the same caliber as most of our tenants and their guests—but I'll vouch for him. He'll only be joining us for a couple of hours anyway."

"If you say it's all right, Mr. Goodman, I'll take your word for it," Billy said. "I just hope no one complains."

Ogden patted Billy on the back. "I assure you there'll be no trouble," he said. "And here's a little something extra for your concern." He handed Billy a fifty-dollar bill. "Why don't you buy that sweet wife of yours some flowers tonight?"

"Thank you, Mr. Goodman," Billy said, tipping his hat with one hand and slipping the bill into his pocket with the other. He hurried to open the door for Ogden, Johnny, Charles, and their guest.

ONCE AGAIN, OGDEN STOOD at the threshold of the condominium. He asked the panhandler to wait outside. Ogden, Johnny, and Charles entered. Johnny unhooked the dog from the leash, and Ogden crept behind Sarah. He put his hands over her eyes and kissed the top of her head. "Darling, turn off the television," he said. "Do I have a surprise for you!"

Sarah fumbled blindly to press the off-button on the remote control. With a touch, a large ocean liner vanished from the screen. "What is it?" she said, a giddy smile on her face. "I love surprises."

"Just you wait and see," Ogden whispered in her ear. He lifted his head and shouted toward the half-opened door. "Good sir, come in!"

Closing the door behind him, the panhandler entered. He was preceded by the acrid scent of body odor, which became pronounced in the enclosed area. Ogden lifted his hands from Sarah's eyes, and Johnny—followed at his heels by Charles—moved closer to the shelter of his mother's arms. The panhandler hesitated near the entryway. Sarah looked at the stranger, then up at Charles behind her. Her mouth agape, she stammered. "Who—who—who is this?" she said.

"Why, Sarah, this man has come to entertain us," Ogden said. "Remember the consternation we so recently expressed at the lack of quality programming available on our television set. This man—for a small fee—will provide us with the story of his life. I call that a bargain."

"But I had just started a movie before you got here," Sarah said.

"What?" Ogden said. "Titanic? Again? We know how that story ends—the urchin dies. Tonight, we will learn something truly meaningful."

"If you say so, honey," Sarah said, her chin sinking to her chest. She fumbled with her hands in her lap.

"Now, where are our manners?" Ogden said, snapping his fingers. "Johnny, get this man a chair. Place it in front of the television set—this area shall be the proscenium."

Johnny slunk to the dining area, pulled one of the black-leather high-back chairs from the table, and set it in front of the television set. Ogden approached the panhandler, who still stood near the doorway, and ushered him to his place. The panhandler sat in the chair. "Would you like a glass of water?" Ogden said.

"Please," the panhandler said. "I'm parched."

"Sarah, would you be so kind as to get this man a glass of water?" Ogden said.

Sarah rose from the sofa, bowed slightly to the man, and proceeded to the kitchen. She lingered in the kitchen briefly. While she was there, Ogden heard her open the kitchen window. He turned to see her approaching with a red plastic-cup of water in her hand. Before returning to the television room, however, she opened the window in the dining area, too.

The family sat on the sofa with Ogden—as usual—centered between his wife and child. Charles, seemingly disturbed by the intruder, neglected his customary place on Ogden's lap and disappeared upstairs. The panhandler, a little wild in the eye, sat silently before them in the chair.

"Johnny," Ogden said, "this man has agreed to entertain us for two hours. You can ask him anything you'd like—same goes for you, Sarah." Ogden gestured to the man. "Sorry, friend. I apologize for the oversight, but please tell us your name?"

The panhandler smiled, revealing a row of battered yellow teeth. "Ozymandias," he said. "Ozymandias, king of kings."

"Ozymandias, eh?" Ogden said. "Now there's a name I haven't heard since Exeter. I guess a good name never dies. But, since that appellation fails to fall trippingly from the tongue, we'll call you 'Ozy' for short." Ogden prodded Johnny by pinching his shoulder. "Johnny, now's your chance. Ask Ozy a question."

"Mr. Ozy," Johnny said, unable to meet the bloodshot stare of the guest, "earlier, in the park, why did you ask my dad for money?"

"Good question, kid," the panhandler answered. "Once upon a time I ruled a mighty kingdom. Now, with my empire crumbled to dust and my wife a mummy somewhere, you could say my family has fallen on hard times."

Sarah raised her hand and waited for the panhandler to acknowledge her. The panhandler nodded to allow her to speak. "Couldn't you get a job somewhere?" she said. "I see lots of opportunities out there. There's a new Starbucks around the corner. And I saw a help-wanted sign at the 24-hour store near the park entrance."

The panhandler pulled a flask from the back pocket of his jeans. He took a swig. "I can't say there's much use for a broken-down pharaoh in these parts of the world," he said. "Wrong place, wrong time, I guess."

The conversation continued like this for some time. Sarah and Johnny proffered earnest questions, and the panhandler provided nonsensical responses. Much to Ogden's chagrin, the evening quickly became a bore—much less interesting than Billy Zane's outrageous antics aboard a sinking ocean liner. Something had to be done.

"Ozy," Ogden said, "we've had enough discussion for now. With one hour passed, I could either pay you half of the agreed sum, or you could entertain us in other ways. Can you dance?"

"Sure, I can dance," the panhandler said. "They used to call me 'the old soft shoe' back in the day."

"Fantastic," Ogden said, smiling. "Get ready to cut a rug." He stepped behind the panhandler to a glass entertainment center, which sat below the television. He scrolled through the song choices on his MP3 player before he located the desired tune. "Bull's-eye," he said as he pressed play.

From the speakers mounted inconspicuously throughout the room, the stirring pluck of a banjo emanated. Ogden clasped his hands to signal his pleasure at hearing one of his favorite childhood songs. The voice of the singer twanged: "I knew a man Bojangles and he'd dance for you / in worn out shoes..."

Ogden hurried back to his seat. "Now, my friend," he said. "Dance!"

The panhandler rose, dusted off his jeans, and tapped his foot in an attempt to find the beat. With an odd undulation rolling from his hips to his shoulders, the panhandler jerked his legs high. The motion emulated a frightened, rearing horse. As his feet returned to the floor, they plodded upon the wood with no connection to the rhythm of the song. Throwing his arms toward the ceiling, the panhandler spun. His eyes bulged and his tongue lolled as he circled aimlessly throughout the room. Ogden and Sarah covered their eyes and laughed. Johnny clapped with cupped hands at the disjointed display. "Mr. Bojangles—Mr. Bojangles," the panhandler howled gruffly with the chorus.

"Dance, dance, dance..." Ogden chanted with the beat. Sarah and Johnny followed Ogden's lead.

Within a few minutes, the song reached its denouement, the banjo faded, and the panhandler dropped to his knees and bowed before the family. The Goodmans applauded. Ogden slapped his knee with delight, and Sarah—so impressed with the performance—briefly forgot about the acrid scent of body odor that hung in the air.

"Yay!" Johnny shouted, grinning from ear to ear.

"Good show, Ozy," Ogden said. "From now on, I dub thee Bojangles."

The panhandler stood and bowed again, this time from the waist. His improvisatory dance was the first display of the hour. Next, Sarah, a sentimentalist at heart, requested that the panhandler pantomime to her favorite song, Send in the Clowns. The panhandler obliged, much to her delight. When the first sounds of the English Horn previewed the song's melody, the panhandler rested his head against his folded hands, opened his eyes, and pretended to wake from a dream. With his tattered clothing, scraggly beard, and red nose, he resembled the famous old-time clown, Emmett Kelly. A tear rolled down Sarah's cheek as the panhandler moved—much more fluidly now—through the large television room. The oddness that had fueled his conversation and subsequent dance disappeared when he faced the sorrow of this song. Clearly, sadness became him, and the family rewarded him with another round of applause at the performance's conclusion.

"Bravo!" Sarah shouted, fighting back additional tears. "Bravo!"

Johnny had enjoyed the melancholy performance but was still a child. He desired something more upbeat. He suggested that the family sing Old MacDonald and that the panhandler emulate the various animals the family would name. He shook with excitement in his seat as he relayed his request.

"Sure thing, Johnny," Ogden said. "I'm sure that's no problem—right, Bojangles?" The panhandler nodded. Ogden asked Johnny to move the chair back to the dining area. "That should give you some room. I suggest you get on all fours, Bojangles. These denizens of the barnyard aren't likely to stand on two feet."

Johnny returned to the sofa after moving the chair. He clapped his hands and tapped his feet. The family followed his lead. "Old MacDonald had a farm / Ee I ee I oh…" Soon the panhandler was crawling about the floor mooing, oinking, and baaing to the various animals the family named. Occasionally, he stood, flapped imaginary wings, and clucked like a chicken or gobbled like a turkey. Johnny populated Mr. MacDonald's farm with a variety of animals that would have made Noah proud. Included along with the standard agricultural fare were elephants, lions, even a Tyrannosaurus. The panhandler performed admirably, attempting even to mimic the sounds of animals of which he had scant knowledge. When he failed, the family booed joshingly—but they heartily hurrahed his successes.

The family continued with the Old MacDonald song for the remainder of the panhandler's time with them. As the second hour ended, Ogden rose from the sofa, held his arms in the air to silence his wife and child, and spoke. "Good friend Bojangles," he said, "please accept our gratitude for your performance." He reached out his hand to the panhandler, who was still crouched on all fours, and helped the man to his feet. The sweaty grime of the panhandler's hand rubbed off on his, and Ogden wiped his hand on his handkerchief to remove the dirt. Sarah and Johnny rose from their seats, bowed their heads to the panhandler, and thanked him for his efforts. The panhandler kicked back one of his legs, looked each member of the family in the eye, and bowed deeply with one arm folded at his stomach and the other folded at his back.

"You're welcome, all of you," the panhandler said, looking around the room as if he were lost. "Now why am I here again?"

Sarah and Johnny looked quizzically at each other. Ogden, on the other hand, guffawed and slapped the panhandler on the back. "Oh, Bojangles," he said, "you're a joker to the end. Come with me. I think I owe you some money. In fact, don't be surprised if you receive a little extra for your troubles. We were quite pleased."

The panhandler took another swig from the flask, mumbled something incomprehensible, and swiveled his head back and forth. Ogden interlocked his arm with the panhandler's, winked over his shoulder at Sarah, and led the panhandler toward the condominium door. Sarah fluttered her eyelids over her bright blue eyes and smiled at Ogden. Ogden saw a glow on her cheeks reminiscent of the glow on the night on which he had proposed to her some ten years ago. He blushed as he and the panhandler walked into the hallway.

"Good night, Bojangles," Johnny shouted from behind the closed door.

THAT NIGHT OGDEN AND Sarah lay in bed. Ogden wore blue wool pajamas, even in the summer, and Sarah wore a pink silk nightgown with a white bow tied across her bosom. She huddled close to Ogden and rested her head on his chest. He crooked his neck and kissed her forehead. He held her tight and whispered to her. "I once heard a man ask, 'Is this the face that launched a thousand ships?'" he said. He kissed her forehead a second time.

She giggled, her button nose moving side-to-side like a bunny rabbit's. "Why do you ask?" she said, batting her eyelashes. "Does something need launching?" She placed her hand on his thigh.

Quickly, Ogden stayed Sarah's hand with his. "N-n-no, my dear," he said. "Nothing like that. I only wished to compare your beauty to a beauty of old. I cherish you dearly."

Sarah removed her hand from Ogden's thigh and draped her arm across his stomach. "I just thought you might want some relief after a long week," she said. "It has been a while—and I thought it might be nice after all the fun we had with Ozymastodon or Bojangles or whatever his name was."

"It hasn't been so long," Ogden said. He gazed at the ceiling and tried to recollect the last time they had had intercourse. "It couldn't have been more than—"

"A month," Sarah said. "It was on the night of my birthday."

"I'm sorry, dear," Ogden said, rubbing his feet together under the covers. "Has it been that long? I'm just so tired most nights."

"It's all right," Sarah said. She sighed. Looking toward Ogden's face, she kissed the cleft in his chin. "I really did have fun tonight."

"It was marvelous," Ogden said. "We'll have to do it again soon." For a moment, he closed his eyes and pondered why he found it so difficult to make love to his wife. Surely, I want no other woman, he thought. I admire Sarah heartily. He did not want to think too long on the matter, though, and, unable to find a convincing reason, he clapped his hands twice. The lights shut off.

"Good night, Ogden," Sarah said.

"Good night, darling," Ogden said.

ON MONDAY MORNING, Ogden sat behind his L-shaped cherry-wood desk and reviewed the contents of the Shakti file. The file contained information regarding the acquisition of one lighting-services company by a larger one, and Ogden's firm had been retained to shepherd the intended transaction through to completion. As Ogden reviewed the smaller company's financials, a junior partner approached Ogden's open office door. The young man stood there looking at his feet. He was slightly taller than Ogden, with a muscular build, dark eyes, and olive-colored skin. Ogden believed him to be of Mexican descent. The man waited at the door, but Ogden—immersed in his review—didn't look up. Eventually, the young man cleared his throat. Ogden raised his eyes from the papers on his desk. "Juan, I didn't know you were waiting," he said.

"I'm sorry to bother you, Mr. Goodman," Juan said, "but Mr. Jones wants to meet with you later for lunch." He continued to look deferentially at his feet.

"No bother at all," Ogden said. "Please instruct Dorothy to put it on my calendar."

"I will, Mr. Goodman," Juan said. "Again, I'm sorry to interrupt you." He turned to walk away.

"Wait," Ogden said, closing the file. He moved from behind his desk and walked toward the door. As a senior partner, he knew he had a responsibility to mentor those beneath his station, and Juan was smart, hard-working, and personable—a real up-and-comer. "There's no need for apologies, Juan. I enjoy a good chat as much as the next fellow." He approached Juan and patted him on the back. "Why don't you sit and speak with me for a while?"

Juan followed Ogden into the office and sat in a leather chair opposite Ogden's desk. From his vantage point, Juan looked past Ogden through the office window at the skyline of a bustling metropolis. Ogden noticed this and glanced over his shoulder to take in the view, which was impressive. Glimmering spires hove toward the heavens, mirrored windows reflected the white summer sunlight, and century-old stone facades lent an air of permanence to the ever-changing city. Level with their eyes, a helicopter flew in the distance over the river. Ogden turned back toward Juan and caught a touch of wonder spreading across the young man's face. Ogden assumed that the world in which Juan now operated was a far cry from the world in which this young man had come of age. With a blink of his eyes, Juan shook his head.

"You have a wonderful office here, Mr. Goodman," Juan said.

"I can see you appreciate it," Ogden said. "It's something to which you may aspire if you continue to work hard. Tell me, now, would you like someday to sit behind a desk like mine in an office like this one?"

"Very much, Mr. Goodman," Juan said. "It would make my family very proud."

"I am quite sure your family is proud of you even now," Ogden said, resting his elbows on his desk and clasping his hands together. "I hear good things about you, Juan. You put in eighty-, ninety-hour weeks—and the quality of your work is excellent. Those things don't go unnoticed. Keep up the effort and you may make senior partner soon."

"I'll do my best, Mr. Goodman," Juan said. "I hope to reward this firm's faith in me."

Ogden looked at his watch. "I have a phone meeting soon, but let's chat again in a few days," he said. He rose from his seat, accompanied Juan to the door, and shook Juan's hand.

"Don't forget to have some fun, though. There are other things in life besides work. By the way, how is that young lady you brought to the Memorial Day party a few weeks ago? She was very pleasant, as I recall."

"Unfortunately, Mr. Goodman, it didn't work out," Juan said. He shrugged his shoulders. "She said I spent too much time at the office."

Ogden patted him on the back. "It's understandable," he said, "but I wouldn't get too distressed about it. A good-looking, ambitious, young man like you will have them lined up a mile long. I can guarantee that."

Juan thanked Ogden again and walked away. Ogden shut the door behind him. He cracked his knuckles and returned to his desk. The phone rang.

AT LUNCH, OGDEN SAT with Roger Jones. Roger was an equity partner in the firm at which Ogden worked. They often met for lunch and talked shop, and today was no different. Roger wanted to know how things with the Shakti acquisition appeared, and Ogden said he had some concerns about the smaller company's profitability. Roger shook his head. "Fools," he said. "I hope they weren't misrepresenting themselves to our client."

Ogden took a sip of his water. "Have no concerns, Roger," he said. "I'll get to the bottom of this."

"You always do," Roger said. He winked at Ogden. "That quality will make you an equity partner soon."

Ogden smiled. He liked Roger, despite the differences in their appearances and personalities. Roger stood a good four inches shorter than Ogden and had gray eyes and white hair. In Ogden's mind, Roger's ostentatious manner of dress mimicked the gaudy displays of the nouveau riche. Moreover, Roger enjoyed his drink, smoked cigars, and had a reputation as a philanderer. Even now, when the server approached them, Roger smoothed his tailored silk suit and adjusted his gold cufflinks. "Listen, doll," he said, raising an eyebrow flirtatiously. "I'll have a martini, and my friend—the teetotaler here—will have a club soda with lime."

The server nodded to both of them.

"Thank you, ma'am," Ogden said.

Roger watched the server as she walked away. Her full hips swayed beneath a tight black skirt. "How'd you like to put your johnson in that?" he said beneath his breath.

Ogden pretended not to hear Roger's comment. Over the years, their families had become friendly, and Ogden deliberately diverted the conversation. "By the way, Roger," he said. "How are Martha and the kids doing these days?"

Roger flicked his hand dismissively. "Don't ask," he said. "It's more of the same. There's nothing I can do to make them happy. We watch TV together—they're bored. We go out to dinner—they're bored. We catch a show downtown—they're bored. I'm at my wit's end. Sometimes, honestly, I wonder how you do it. You, Sarah, and Johnny always seem so happy."

"Well, Roger," Ogden said, smiling, "maybe I can be of some assistance. I'll let you in on a little secret. I think I may have stumbled upon a way to relieve your family's boredom." He leaned forward and motioned for Roger to come closer.

Ogden whispered in Roger's ear.

THE REST OF THE WEEK passed uneventfully. As usual, Ogden left for work at seven in the morning and returned home at seven or eight at night. By the time he came home in the evening, Sarah and Johnny had already eaten and dismissed Maria until the following day. For dinner, Ogden reheated the food Maria had prepared, placed a folding wooden TV tray in front of the couch, and ate while his family watched television. Sarah and Johnny still sat on either side of him, and Charles continued to dance around his feet—but something had changed. As Ogden flipped from one channel to the next, he broadcast his dissatisfaction with the evening's primetime options. Now, however, Sarah and Johnny, too, heaped their derision on their formerly beloved companion. On Thursday night, after three consecutive evenings of disappointment, the family's frustration boiled over.

That night, Ogden, pork chop in one hand and remote control in the other, clicked from channel to channel. It was more of the same. On the first channel, a hard-boiled detective told his wisecracking partner that he would take down the Varano family—no matter what. On another, two quirky city slickers set out to run a general store in a rural New England town—with hilarious results. On yet another, a game-show host asked two buxom females to eat a plate crawling with worms—to the groans of a studio audience. With each successive switch, Ogden's thumb thudded more forcefully against the remote control. He shook his head, closed his eyes, and gritted his teeth. "I do not understand how this is happening," he said. He shut off the television, slammed the remote control down beside him, and rested his head in the palm of his hand. "Am I insane—or has the television become a hub for inanity?"

"You're not insane," Sarah said, placing her arm across Ogden's shoulders. "I don't understand how we used to watch this drivel."

Johnny, unused to such expressions of frustration from his parents, put his arms around his father's torso. "Don't worry, Mommy and Daddy," he said. "It will be OK. This dumb TV is double stupid."

Then, with the television no longer warbling in the background, the room fell into utter silence. No one spoke for minutes. Even Charles stopped wagging the tiny nub of his tail and sat still on the floor in front of the sofa. Each family member blankly stared at the black screen in front of them. Ogden, in particular, struggled to understand what had happened. He lowered his head, clasped his hands together, and spoke in a low voice. "This television has had a good run," he said, "but I think it's time we avail ourselves of other entertainment opportunities."

"I agree, honey," Sarah said. She removed her arm from Ogden's shoulders, placed her hand in his, and leaned against him. "To think I was ready to sit through Titanic for the tenth time last week—it boggles the mind."

Johnny's eyes lit up as he listened. He bounced in his seat and patted his hands together. "Do you think we could invite Ozy back, Daddy?" he said.

Ogden tousled the hair of his towheaded son. "I don't think that will be feasible, Johnny," he said. "I fear our friend Ozymandias may have returned at last to his faraway kingdom—if not in body, then in mind. But I might be able to find another Ozymandias if that would please you. Would you like that, Johnny?"

Johnny looked at the ceiling and seemed to ponder his father's question. "Would another Ozy dance and make animal sounds?" he said.

"Sure, he would, Johnny," Ogden said. "He'd do whatever you'd like. Money will make people quite amenable to all kinds of requests."

Johnny bounced in his seat again. "Please, Daddy," he said. "Please bring home another Ozy."

"I will do my best, son," Ogden said. He unclasped his hand from Sarah's and put his arm around her. "Darling, is there anything you would like our next entertainer to do?"

Sarah brushed her hair from her eyes and kissed Ogden on the cheek. She blushed slightly and voiced a lingering concern. "There's nothing in particular I'd really like him to do," she said. "But is it possible to find someone who may have bathed more recently? It took until Maria disinfected this room on Monday to rid it of Ozy's odor."

Ogden pinched Sarah's nose. "I'd say you have the nose of a bloodhound, darling, but this little button is much too cute to be compared to a canine's proboscis," he said.

Sarah giggled and pushed Ogden's hand from her face. "Stop," she said. "That tickles."

"Whatever you say, my dear," Ogden said. "I'll even sniff under his arms if I must." He pulled his wife and son close. "We'll have fun tomorrow night as a family. I guarantee it."

THE FOLLOWING EVENING, Ogden arrived home early, around five o'clock. His family greeted him at the door, and Maria set the table for dinner. "Mr. Goodman," she said, "I made another one of your favorites tonight. Can you guess what?"

"Hmmm," Ogden said, "last week it was ham and mashed potatoes—delicious fare. Could it be macaroni and cheese with coleslaw tonight?"

"Good guess, Mr. Goodman," Maria said, "but it's hamburgers con queso—I mean, with cheese—and tater tots. Is that OK?"

"More than OK," Ogden said. "You know how I enjoy our national contributions to world cuisine." He patted Maria on her shoulder. "You never fail to come through, Maria. You truly are a culinary marvel."

Maria blushed, her bronze cheeks gathering a roselike hue. "Thank you, Mr. Goodman," she said.

"De nada, my dear," Ogden said. "Now let's eat."

The family and Maria gathered at the table in the same formation in which they had sat the previous week. Ogden folded his hands near his chest, bowed his head, and said grace. After a resounding "Amen," Maria served them, and they commenced to eat. Even Charles, who sat patiently beside Ogden's seat, received a quarter of a burger from his doting master. Once their bellies were full, they conversed freely. At first, Ogden spoke about some of his issues with the Shakti project, but he and Sarah also talked to Johnny about the upcoming school week, which would be Johnny's last before summer vacation. Maria then turned the conversation toward their evening plans.

"Are you doing anything special tonight?" Maria said.

"I believe we intend to have a guest over," Ogden said.

Maria smiled nervously and fidgeted with her hair, which she wore tonight in a tight bun.

"Don't worry, Maria," Sarah said. "I already spoke to Ogden about it. We'll make sure our friend has bathed more recently this time around."

AFTER DINNER, OGDEN wandered the streets around the park. He asked himself where he could find a clean but desperate man eager to earn a buck. The options seemed limited. At one corner, a promising young man with light hair and light eyes occupied a prime piece of panhandling real estate—but he whirled in place and conversed with himself. About halfway down the next street, an elderly Asian man with a Fu Manchu moustache held out a can and begged for money—but he stank of urine and stale cigarettes. Still farther down the street, an overweight middle-aged man with dark sunglasses and a trench coat leaned against a wall with a "Will work for food" sign hanging from his neck—but he engaged the passersby too familiarly, especially small blonde-haired boys. Frustrated, Ogden looked east and west, north and south, but to no avail. Where can I turn? he thought.

Ogden then remembered that an old YMCA still existed across the park. They have showers there—and desperate people, he thought. He hastened to the building, eager to arrive before twilight fell. After wending across several of the paths that ran near the lake in the park, he angled himself toward 63rd Street on the city's west side. At the YMCA, he stood outside the gray-stone façade and waited. The arched entryway contained decaying decorative woodworking that harked back to a once impressive past. Unfortunately, the entryway now mirrored the fading glory of its inhabitants, who appeared beneath its arc in various stages of sartorial disrepair. Some wore mustard-stained shorts, others donned ripped jeans, and all wore greasy, sweat-ringed T-shirts. Landscapers' attire, Ogden thought. Dressed in his monogrammed beige suit and white silk shirt, he cut a stark contrast with the building's inhabitants. "Now how do I approach these fellows," he asked himself, "without appearing eager for some unsavory shenanigans?"

As Ogden connived a reason to speak with one of the loitering residents of the YMCA, a voice called from the sidewalk behind him. "Yo, slick," it said. Ogden spun around and saw a grinning black man wearing a purple fedora and mustard-colored suit. A pencil-thin moustache topped his smile, and he sat on a small stool behind an upside-down cardboard box upon which a stack of cards rested. The man picked up the cards and shuffled them effortlessly.

"Were you calling to me, my good man?" Ogden said.

The man crooked his neck and looked at Ogden with one eye closed. "What kind of question is that?" he said. "Who else here besides us looks slick? I sure as hell wasn't calling to myself."

"Touché," Ogden said, dusting off his shoulders and walking toward the man. "Point well taken. And what, pray tell, are you doing here?"

"You ever play Three-card Monte, slick?" the man said, placing three cards face down on the box. "You just follow the cards, follow the cards."

Ogden watched the man's hands intently as the man revealed the center card as the ace of spades, turned it face down, and passed the three cards swiftly over one another until he lifted the ace of spades unexpectedly from his left-hand side. Ogden appeared stupefied. "This game in no way resembles Contract Bridge," he said.

"Contract Bridge—what the hell you talking about, slick?" the man said. "The only bridges around here are the George Washington, Brooklyn, and Triborough. For this game, all you have to do is put some money down, and, if you guess where the ace of spades is, I pay you out—it's an easy way to double your cash."

"Three-card Monte, eh?" Ogden said. "I didn't retain my wealth by playing games of chance—unless you call playing the market a game of chance." He laughed at his joke and slapped the side of his leg. "Oh, that's a knee-slapper."

The man stared dumbfounded at Ogden. "Yeah, real funny, slick," he said. "I can see you're too smart for this game—but how'd you like a piece of the action? You look perfect for what I have in mind. All you need to do is stand here and pretend you're playing. I let you win a few games so that people passing by think they have a shot too. I'll call them over to play, then we reel them in." The man smiled and acted like he were reeling in a heavy fish with an imaginary pole. "What do you think, slick?"

Ogden looked the man in the eye. "The old rope-a-dope," he said. "I like your initiative, my friend. And what, if you don't mind me asking, would I receive for my exertions?"

"The standard ten percent, slick," the man said.

Ogden felt in his element again, and his pulse quickened. "Ten percent of what amount?" he said.

The man looked Ogden up and down. "A clean-cut gentleman like yourself, and an enterprising salesman like me—we could bring in two-hundred or two-fifty in a couple of hours."

"Yet I would only earn twenty to twenty-five dollars for my labor," Ogden said, shaking his head. "I hardly call that worth my effort."

The man looked toward the sky, rubbed his chin, and shuffled his feet behind the box. "Now let's see," he said, "maybe we could—" He raised the brim of his fedora slightly as beads of sweat formed on his forehead. He seemed to know he was losing his opportunity.

Not wishing to make the man suffer, Ogden rubbed his hands together and cleared his throat. "There's no need for further negotiation on this topic, my good man," he said. "I didn't come to the foot of this noble institution to play the shill in a conman's game. Yet, if you'd like to earn two hundred and fifty dollars for two hours of work, I may be able to assist you." He considered his offer fair, in light of the man's sterling appearance and entrepreneurial disposition.

The man leaned from side to side and sized Ogden up. "I should have known," he said, chuckling. "A Fifth-Avenue type like you likes the gutter boys. I saw you sizing up those lads earlier. You with your sandy hair just so, and your Robert Redford smile—you must drive the poor boys crazy. But, just so we're clear, I'm not one for backdoor shenanigans or gerbil games. You'll have to find someone else for that—in fact, I could probably assist you in that search—for a finder's fee."

Ogden sighed, lowered his head, and struck his hand against his forehead. "No, no, no," he said. "I seek the purchase of no unwholesome services. I merely wish to contract for two hours of clean family entertainment."

The man stood up. He was about half a foot shorter than Ogden and had no stink about him. He played with the collar of his purple dress shirt, which matched the color of his hat. "Keep talking," he said. "I'm listening."

Ogden rested his hand on the man's shoulder, leaned close to him, and explained his proposition.

OUTSIDE OF HIS CONDOMINIUM, Ogden once again greeted Billy, the doorman. In the gloaming, the last light of the setting sun fell upon the building's smooth granite exterior, bathing it in a pink glow. As Billy held the door for Ogden and his guest, Billy stared at his feet. This time, Billy asked no questions, and Ogden handed him a generous tip. Ogden presumed Billy had no issue with his guest due to his guest's well-groomed appearance. Yet, as Ogden and the man walked through the vestibule past his neighbors, the McClellans, he heard Mary McClellan comment under her breath to her husband, "George, did you see that man with Ogden?"

Her husband responded with no attempt to mask his displeasure. "There goes the neighborhood, dear," he said. "I told you we should have moved to Westport when we had the chance."

At the elevator door, Ogden apologized to his guest. "I'm sorry, my friend, for the antebellum views of some residents of this building," he said. "I am sad to say that it is often hard to find privilege without prejudice."

"Fuck that shit," the man said, adjusting his grip on the box that held his stool and cards. "I'm here for two-hundred-and fifty dollars—not a march from Selma to Montgomery."

Ogden straightened his collar and tapped his foot. The elevator seemed to be taking longer than usual. "I appreciate your understanding, my friend," he said. "But I must ask you to refrain from such salty language when we are upstairs. My son has yet to reach six years of age."

"No problem, slick," the man said. "What's your name, anyway?"

"Ogden," Ogden said. "Ogden Goodman. And yours?"

"Willie," the man said. "Willie Russell."

"Nice to meet you, Willie," Ogden said, extending his hand. The two men shook hands as the elevator door opened.

They stepped inside.

OGDEN OPENED THE CONDOMINIUM door and beamed as he introduced Willie to his family. He felt proud of his generous and welcoming nature. If you include Maria, I now am assisting two persons of color, he thought. Sarah smiled at Ogden, took Willie's box, and placed it against the wall next to the media center. She then returned to Willie—with Johnny in tow—and shook his hand. Johnny, hunching, tensed his shoulders when he grasped the hand of the stranger. Afterward, he tugged on his mother's houndstooth skirt.

"He doesn't look like Ozy," Johnny said.

"No," Sarah said, sizing Willie up. "But he dresses well and smells clean—and I bet he can dance."

Willie stepped forward, crouched, and patted Johnny on his head. "Hey, kid," he said. "I think I could sharpen up that outfit of yours." He placed his purple fedora on Johnny's head. The hat drooped to the side and covered one of Johnny's eyes. "Now you look slick—like your pops." Johnny stood speechless, his hands in the pockets of his white shorts. Wearing his blue polo shirt with his prep school's emblem and the purple fedora, he looked one part young Rockefeller, another part aspiring pimp.

Ogden pinched his son's ruddy cheek. "Johnny, you little rapscallion," he said. "Give our man Willie back his hat. He may require it for his premiere performance."

Johnny took the hat from his head and held it in front of Willie. "Here, Mr. Willie," he said. "Daddy wants you to have your hat back."

Willie set the hat on his head. It covered a short, well-groomed afro. "Ogden, you should be proud," he said. "I wish any one of my sons were so polite."

Ogden took Johnny into his arms. "Love and respect for others—of all backgrounds—breed good manners," he said.

The family, followed by Willie, adjourned to the television area. As they approached the sofa, Charles, who had been sitting there unseen, beat a hasty retreat upstairs. Ogden placed Johnny on the recently vacated cushion, and Sarah sat far enough from her son to leave space between them for Ogden. Willie removed his jacket and draped it over the side of his box. Ogden fumbled with the MP3 player, searching for one of his favorite songs.

Willie, taking his place in the center of the television area, rolled up his sleeves and made circles in the air with his outstretched arms. His supple movements intimated a lean and limber frame. He touched his toes and stretched his legs as if he were preparing for a sprint. "You ready, slick," he said to Ogden. "It'll be just the way we planned it."

"Just a moment," Ogden said, still fumbling with the MP3 player. "Almost there." He looked over his shoulder at his family. "I believe we are in for quite a treat. Our friend here told me earlier that he's an aficionado of the old electric boogaloo." When he found the song he wanted, he pressed play. The first scratches sounded from the speakers, and the percussion kicked in. Ogden snapped his fingers to the pulsing strains of Herbie Hancock's Rockit as he hurried to sit between his wife and son.

Willie instantly started popping and locking to the heavy syncopation. Ogden clapped to the beat, and Sarah oohed. With his hands on his cheeks and his mouth open wide, Johnny stared in fascination. "He dances like a robot, daddy!" he said. Then, in synchronization with the thrust of the throbbing synthesizers, Willie tossed his hat into his box and dropped to the floor. From there, he turtled, six-stepped, and flared, flowing seamlessly from one move to the next.

"That man has some rhythm," Sarah said.

"They're gifted that way," Ogden said, applauding Willie's perfectly executed transition to the worm.

"Wow! The voice in the song even sounds like a robot!" Johnny said.

As the song transitioned into a segment heavy with scratching, Willie jumped to his feet and moonwalked across the wood floor. The family gaped in awe. Willie smiled and winked at them. Anticipating the song's crescendo, he returned to the floor, rolled through three windmills, and curled into a rapid back spin. Timing his final movement with the conclusion of the song, he stretched lengthwise on his side, resting his cheek on his left hand. The stylized ending impressed all who watched it and capped a sterling performance. Ogden rose from his seat and signaled his family to stand beside him. "Bravo!" he shouted. "Bravo!"

Willie stood, wiped the sweat from his brow, and bowed to the family. "You're too kind," he said.

"Willie," Sarah said, staring dumbfounded, "where did you learn this electric jigaboo?"

"What the f—" Willie said. He screwed up his eyes. "What did you say? Are you kidding me? Ogden, tell me she didn't really say that."

"Did I say something wrong?" Sarah said, glancing at Ogden and then casting her eyes downward.

"I'm sorry, Willie," Ogden said. "Sarah merely misspoke. It could happen to anyone." He took Sarah's hand in his. "Sarah, my dear, it's called electric boogaloo."

"Oh gosh," Sarah said, raising her eyes to meet Willie's. "I apologize. I truly meant no offence."

Willie bit his lower lip, looked at Sarah askance, and guffawed. He slapped Ogden on his back. "You're a lucky man," he said. "The way your wife flashes those baby blues and flutters those long lashes of hers—I would have forgiven her if she had called me 'darkie.' You're just lucky O.J. didn't meet her first. He would have snatched this blondie up right away."

Sarah giggled nervously.

With a faraway look in his eye, Ogden released Sarah's hand. He turned toward the window in the dining area, gazing beyond the fluorescent glow emanating from the streetlamps below. As a lifelong fan of the Buffalo Bills, he often felt a touch of sorrow when his childhood hero was mentioned. "The Juice," he said, "—now there is a true American tragedy. I often think I should offer him my services, pro bono, to attempt to free him from his unjust and undignified incarceration. For Christ's sake, the man rushed two thousand and three yards in a fourteen-game season."

"Please, honey, don't take the Lord's name in vain," Sarah said, placing her hand on Ogden's shoulder. "Not with Johnny around."

"Whoopish!" Willie said, snapping his wrist and emulating the sound of a cracking whip. "I can see who wears the pants in this family. I'll bet she's a real tiger in the sack, too. It's always the quiet, innocent-looking ones."

Sarah blushed.

Johnny, still standing by Ogden's side, screwed up his eyes. "Daddy, why would Mommy be a tiger in a sack?" he said.

"Oh, son," Ogden said, patting Johnny on the head, "sometimes grown-ups say silly, meaningless things—much like children do. Pay no attention to them. No one's becoming a tiger here." He asked his family to sit down. "We could stand here jabbering all evening, or we could watch another one of Willie's fine performances. Sarah, why don't you choose what you would like Willie to do next?" Sarah and Johnny resumed their places on the sofa, and Ogden headed toward the kitchen. "Willie, would you like a glass of water?"

Willie said yes, and Ogden returned from the kitchen with a glass tumbler of water. "Thank you," Willie said.

While Ogden took his seat, Sarah scrunched her eyes and rubbed her hands in her lap. She appeared deep in thought. "I don't know," she said aloud. "There are so many great artists to choose from." She sat back in her seat and ran her hands through her hair. Suddenly, her face brightened. "I know—I know. Are you familiar with any songs by Lionel Richie?"

"The chief Commodore himself?" Willie said. "Of course, I know his songs. What do you think I was—born yesterday?"

"What about Hello?" Sarah said. "Could you lip-synch to that one? It's such a beautiful song."

"Lucky for you," Willie said, "that's one of my girlfriend's favorites. I think I could pull that off. I'm just glad you didn't ask for Running with the Night. I'm pretty tired after all that dancing."

Ogden went to the media center to find the song his wife had requested. At the push of a button, a tender crooning filled the room. Willie pretended to hold a microphone close to his mouth. His lips moved silently to the words. As the song progressed with a slow, steady beat and flowing synthesizer lines, Willie drifted across the floor. He locked eyes with Sarah, treating her as if she were the only person in the room. When the stirring, acoustic-guitar solo began, he reached for her, led her from her seat, and danced briefly with her in the center of the television area. Before the solo ended, he spun her around. Her skirt and hair fanned as she twirled, and she looked the picture of wholesome beauty. Willie returned her to her seat, reclaimed his invisible microphone, and, when the singing resumed, silently cried, "Hello, is it me you're looking for?"

Ogden grinned at his wife, who—with her cheeks lightly flushed—perspired slightly. Tears welled in her eyes, and she applauded vigorously at the song's conclusion.

Ogden reveled at what seemed like another successful evening. The performances of this and the previous week had moved Sarah more than any television show or movie had, and Johnny—grinning and kicking the sofa with the backs of his legs—eagerly awaited his chance to direct Willie's next performance. Even Willie — whether motivated by money or the Goodman family's accolades — appeared deeply satisfied. With his hands clasped behind his head, he stood—rings of sweat darkening his dress shirt beneath his armpits — and anticipated the next request from the audience. He waited no longer than a few seconds.

"Old MacDonald! Old MacDonald!" Johnny shouted.

Willie looked puzzled and fixed his eyes on Ogden.

"Willie," Ogden said, "last week, our performer made the sounds of various barnyard animals while we sang the Old MacDonald song. Johnny would like a repeat performance—with you at the helm. Are you familiar with this song?"

"You got to be kidding me," Willie said. "Old MacDonald—that's one honky-ass song. What comes after that? Mammy? I ain't getting down on my hands and knees and baying like a plantation owner's bloodhound—not for your or anyone else's money."

"Willie, be reasonable," Ogden said. "We mean no disrespect. The Old MacDonald song is fun for persons of all ages."

As Ogden spoke, Johnny dismounted from the sofa. He stamped his feet on the floor. "I knew he wasn't like Ozy," he said. "I want my Old MacDonald! Daddy, make this man play Old MacDonald!"

"Johnny, I can't make Willie do something he doesn't want to do," Ogden said. "You can choose another song for him. Maybe—"

"Make him, Daddy!" Johnny said. "You paid him. He should do whatever I want!"

"Ogden, this kid's got to learn that a man isn't bought and sold like chattel—not in this day and age," Willie said, his arms akimbo.

Johnny's face grew red. He clenched his fist and lowered his forehead. With a shout, he ran at Willie and kicked him in the shin. "Play Old MacDonald!" he screamed.

Mortified, Ogden grabbed Johnny under his arms and set him on the sofa. "Stay there, young lad!" he commanded. He hurried to Willie's side. "I apologize for my son's ignominious outburst. Are you injured, Willie?"

Willie rubbed his shin. "What the—God damn!" he said. "That kid has a boot like Pele. You better hope I'm not hurt. I could sue."

Ogden guided Willie to the other side of the room and paused near the entryway. Johnny cried on the sofa as Sarah reprimanded him.

Ogden knew he had to mitigate the situation before it got out of hand. "Pipe down, Johnny," he ordered.

Johnny stopped crying.

To evince his seriousness to Willie, Ogden put his hand on Willie's shoulder, apologized profusely, and sweetened the evening's deal. "Due to my son's unfortunate behavior, I would like to increase your evening's wages by one-hundred dollars," he said.

Willie shook his head and smiled a brilliant smile. His eyes twinkled beneath the bright light under which they now stood. "You ain't getting off that easy, slick," he said. "You never warned me that your kid was a firecracker about to blow. I need at least five Benjamins to stick around."

"Five-hundred dollars?" Ogden said. "That's a lot of Three-card Monte." He rubbed his chin and let his eyes wander upward. "And, if I accept this counteroffer, there'll be no more discussion of lawsuits or the like."

"No doubt," Willie said. "I can already feel the pain leaving my shin."

"Good," Ogden said. "And you intend to stay for the entire two hours?"

"For five-hundred dollars I will," Willie said. "But I still ain't playing no Old MacDonald."

"Understood," Ogden said, holding out his hand to Willie. "We have a deal then."

"Damn straight," Willie said.

The two men shook hands before turning to face Sarah and Johnny. Their deal consummated, they returned to the television area.

Sarah continued to discipline Johnny in a low voice, threatening him with grounding. "How would you like not to be able to go to your friend's sleepover next weekend," she said. Johnny looked downcast, his cheeks wet with tears. His chin sunk to his chest. Sarah pushed Johnny to apologize. "Now what are you going to say to our friend Willie, young man?"

"I'm sorry, Mr. Willie," Johnny said. He rose to his feet and bowed his head. "Please forgive me for being naughty."

"You better truly be sorry, Johnny," Ogden said. "How would you like it if someone kicked Charlie? I bet you wouldn't be happy about that."

"That's enough for me," Willie said. "The boy said he's sorry. Everyone makes mistakes." He crouched by Johnny's side and whispered in the boy's ear. "Now, what do we have here?" he said, with a quizzical look in his eyes. He reached into Johnny's shirt collar and produced a joker card.

Johnny looked at the card, then back at Willie. "How'd you do that?" he said. "That card wasn't there before."

"Willie is a genius when it comes to prestidigitation," Ogden said. "In fact, when I met him earlier this evening, he was performing a trick they call the 'Three-card Monte.' Perhaps, if you're a good boy, he'll perform this trick for you."

"Willie, please, please, please show me the Three-card Monte trick," Johnny said. He clutched his hands to his chest and bounced up and down. "I bet it's better than that stupid Old MacDonald game."

"I couldn't agree more with that last statement," Willie said, standing up from his crouching position. "But, if you want me to show you the trick, you have to promise to be a good boy the rest of the night."

"I promise—I promise," Johnny said, still bouncing up and down.

"Well, then, let me set up my box," Willie said.

Willie retrieved his box from beneath the television, set up his cards, and began his trick. Johnny sat across from him and oohed and aahed. Sarah and Ogden returned to the sofa, but, this time, they pressed close to each other as they watched their son attempt to unlock the mystery of Willie's movements. Sarah rested her head on Ogden's shoulder, turning her neck to kiss his cheek. He smiled and clutched her hand in his. From the stairwell, a shuffling sounded. Charles poked his head into sight, cocked his ears, and scurried down the remaining steps. He skirted the space Willie and Johnny occupied and jumped onto Ogden's lap. His nubby tail flicked from side to side as Ogden petted his rump.

"Isn't this the life?" Ogden whispered into Sarah's ear. "We truly are blessed."

"Thank you, darling, for everything," she said. "This evening is magical. I just hope Johnny doesn't become spoiled."

The evening's entertainment continued. Ogden and Sarah cheered when Willie showed Johnny how to produce an ace from his shirt pocket. Sarah even participated later, picking cards from the deck for card-counting and other tricks. The night's activities included no further outbursts, and Willie left duly remunerated. Johnny hugged him before he left.

IN THE DARKNESS OF their bedroom, Sarah struggled to sleep. She kissed Ogden on his neck until his snoring stopped. He turned away from her in his sleep, but she persisted. She pushed her chest against his back and guided her hand beneath his pajama top. Twirling her fingers in the tuft of chest hair at his sternum, she nibbled on the back of his ear.

"Don't do that," Ogden mumbled, still sleeping. "That's what naughty girls do."

"Oh, Ogden, please wake up," Sarah said. "I can't sleep." She guided her lips from his earlobe to his nape and nibbled where the shoulder blade meets the neck. "It's all right to be naughty sometimes."

Ogden's eyes opened to the near blackness of the room. He felt the groping at his chest and turned toward Sarah. "Darling, please, not now," he said. "I'm tired." He kissed her lightly on the lips. "I was already fast asleep—such strange dreams."

Sarah removed her hand from beneath his top. She wrapped her arms around him. "Are you sure there's nothing wrong?" she said. "We used to be naughty more often."

"Darling, I'm sorry," Ogden said. He imagined the look of sadness Sarah wore and chastised himself for neglecting his matrimonial duties. "With my obligations at the firm and the opportunity to become an equity partner, I feel a bit out of sorts. Just give me time—maybe next weekend we can. Isn't Johnny going to a sleepover?"

"Yes, he is," Sarah said, her voice rising with anticipation. "It's his last week of school, and he's staying over Tommy's house on Friday night."

Ogden pulled Sarah close to him. "I promise I'll make it up to you then," he said. "I wouldn't want my little butterfly to roam."

Sarah slapped Ogden's behind playfully. "Don't even joke about that," she said. "You know I'm yours and yours alone."

"And I am yours alone," Ogden said. He rubbed the sleep from his eyes. As his eyes acclimated to the darkness, a faint glow colored the room a deep green, but Ogden still could see little. He felt Sarah pull away from him and lie on her back. "Did you enjoy the entertainment tonight?" he asked.

"I did—very much," she said. "But Johnny's behavior surprised me. I haven't seen him kick anyone before. Never." A silence settled briefly between them. A siren on the street below shattered it. Sarah questioned Ogden. "Do you think it's all right?"

"To kick another human being?" Ogden said. "Of course not. I would never condone such behavior. It's textbook assault."

"No, not that," she said. "I was thinking of something else. Do you think it's all right to pay someone to come here and dance for us—or play games for our child?"

"Are you concerned about that?" Ogden said. He turned to face her. He could faintly trace her silhouette. "Both Bojangles and Willie were fairly compensated—and either could have left at any time."

"Yes, but they have little," she said, "and would likely do most anything for money."

"My little butterfly," Ogden said, stroking Sarah's hair. "I always loved you for your compassion. But think of this. The fallacy in your statement arises when you say that Bojangles or Willie would likely do anything for money. Why—just tonight—our man Willie refused to play the Old MacDonald game. And, after a brief, but unfortunate incident, he negotiated new terms to his agreement, and all was well. No one forced him to do anything."

"I guess you're right," Sarah said. "I just don't want Johnny to grow up thinking he can buy people to do the things he wants."

"Sarah, darling," Ogden said, "there is nothing wrong with purchasing someone's services." He kissed Sarah on the cheek. "Think of it this way. A man like Willie comes to our home. He sees the granite façade outside, the Spartan comfort of our living space, and the love our family freely shares. He executes a stellar performance and earns more than a yeoman's wages—then he tells himself, 'If I just work hard, I, too, can find success like this—I, too, can someday dwell in a magnificent space and pay someone to perform for me.'"

"I hadn't thought of it that way before," Sarah said. "I guess I don't feel so bad now."

"I hope that was all that was troubling you, and you can now get some rest," Ogden said. "If anything, we are benefactors of the downtrodden—not their oppressors." He wrapped his arms around his wife, kissed her soft cheek, and fell asleep once more.

Sarah yawned, rolled her head to tease a kink out of her neck, and closed her eyes. She slept soundly until the morning.

OGDEN'S STRANGE DREAMS returned when he fell back asleep. Ever since his youth—especially during periods of stress—he dreamed a recurring dream that recalled an incident that occurred when he was twelve-years-old. During the incident, he discovered what men and women do when they desire one another. The incident defined what he believed to be naughty behavior and crystallized that naughtiness was something best left to the help.

Soon after his eyes closed, Ogden's fitful twisting and turning slowed. His head twitched suddenly, and he mumbled something incomprehensible. He settled on his back, and his body ceased to move. The muscles in his cheeks relaxed, his mouth hung slack, and he entered a deep REM sleep. Within seconds, he was transported to a late-summer evening where the scent of dogwood lingered in the air.

There, Ogden wandered through his family's backyard, slapping a fallen oak branch against his open palm. He had had a brief row with his father, a well-respected judge, who had grown cross with him for fumbling the declension of the Latin verb sum. A crow cawed from a nearby elm, and the young

Ogden trod heavily, his eyes closed and his hand continuing to bear the brunt of the steady strike of his makeshift switch. While he walked, he repeated over and over, "sum, to be; sum, I am; es, you are; est, he, she, it is; sumus, we are; estis, you are, plural; sunt, they are..." He shook his head and wondered why he had had such difficulty minutes ago, when he had botched the declension under the stern eyes of his father.

In the dream, it was a warm spring day, and, as Ogden opened his eyes and looked up from his raw hand, he noticed a yellow bulb beneath an open window near the servant's quarters. A gardener's rake rested against the wall, and a small patch of dirt had recently been agitated. Delighted to see the first crocus of the year, Ogden hurried to take a closer look. The quarters housed the family's maid, Consuela, who doubled as his nanny, and he was eager to tell her of his find.

As Ogden knelt in the grass by the freshly aerated soil and admired the bloom, he heard unfamiliar sounds coming from the window above him. He recognized the sounds as two voices—one familiar, one unfamiliar. The deeper, unknown voice mimicked porcine grunts, and the higher voice—the voice of Ogden's beloved Consuela — rhythmically responded with passionate moans.

Ogden dropped the oak branch he still held, rose from his knees to his tiptoes, and peered over the top of the windowsill. At the foot of Consuela's bed, the sturdy gardener, Hector, stood behind the bent-over maid. With his soil-stained jeans at his ankles, Hector thrust what Ogden referred to as his "pee-pee" deep into his nanny. Consuela, her skirt raised to reveal her ample behind, clutched the sheets, stared straight ahead with an open mouth, and groaned.

"¡Dios mío!" Consuela shouted repeatedly.

Ogden fell back to his knees. He knew not what to do. Is Hector harming Consuela? he wondered. As he wondered, he noticed a strange tingling between his legs. He touched the front of his shorts and felt something he had never felt before. His own pee-pee was hard, much like Hector's.

What's happening? Ogden thought. His mind raced with a mixture of guilt, fear, and excitement. In the heat of the moment, he raced from the servant's quarters across the lawn and up the back steps of his house's porch. His father sat on a bench there, a worn Latin-language copy of Livy's History of Rome in his hands. Panting, Ogden approached his father. Uncertain as to whether Consuela's cries were cries of pleasure or cries of pain, Ogden felt he needed to tell someone. He recounted what he had seen.

His father adjusted his gray tie, tugged at his white moustache, and stared at the servant's quarters with cold blue eyes. He placed his book beside him, straightened his jacket, and stood erect. "You wait here, son," he said. Slowly, he descended the steps to the yard, muttering under his breath, "You can't leave these people alone for more than a few minutes. They're like rabbits."

Ogden woke from his dream. He stared again into the darkness. Sarah's measured breaths hummed from the space beside him, and he pictured her chest rising and falling slowly as she breathed in and out. Instinctively, he placed his hand on his crotch. As usual, the vision of Ogden's beloved Consuela indulging in carnal pleasures had brought his member to full salute. However, memories of that day, many years ago, had blended his first feelings of sexual excitement with profound guilt. For, when his father had returned from the servant's quarters, he had ordered Ogden to his room and commanded Ogden never to speak of the incident again. Later that evening, when Ogden had returned downstairs for supper, he had learned the inevitable—that Consuela had been let go. Hector had not even been mentioned.

From that distant day forward, Ogden's nannies had been matronly gray-haired spinsters who wore their hair in tight buns. To the present day, Ogden held himself responsible for Consuela's misfortune—and was left to ponder a final erotic image of her etched indelibly upon his mind.

As Ogden lay in bed that night, his erection subsiding, he recounted the vision one more time. Is there a way I can turn this unfortunate childhood incident to my advantage? he thought. Perhaps I can muster my memories of that woebegone day and use them as an aid to fulfill my duties to Sarah. He closed his eyes and scratched the back of his neck. Soon thereafter, he had an idea.

THE FOLLOWING MONDAY, when Ogden returned to work, a message from Roger awaited him on his desk. "Come to my office first thing this morning—big news!" it read. Ogden stared at the pink piece of paper and wondered what it could mean. The Shakti acquisition was still in its infancy, so he anticipated nothing new regarding that transaction. He turned to face the window behind him and, for a moment, gazed upon the city. He fumbled with the note in his hand and watched a black-hulled cargo ship pass from the mouth of the river into the open sea. Stacked high on the ship's deck were red, blue, and green containers. All of those items loaded by stevedores upon the briny metal like toy Legos stacked by a child on a soiled floor, he thought. He wondered whether the distant ship carried any goods from companies for which he had provided his services. His work, albeit often arcane and cerebral, had far-reaching consequences for many persons. Executives, middle managers, and union workers all owed him a debt of gratitude for his labor on their companies' acquisitions. Yet, they'll never know a thing that I do, he realized.

When the spell of this brief reverie broke, Ogden remembered Roger's request. He didn't want to keep his friend and mentor waiting. He tightened the Windsor knot at his neck, smoothed out the few creases in his blazer, and disposed of the crumpled note in the trash. He walked from his office eager to embrace the rigors of a new week—and to learn more of this mysterious "news."

As Ogden approached the threshold to Roger's office, Roger called him inside. "Just the man I wanted to see," he said, rising from his leather chair. "You're a godsend, Ogden. It's your idea that may have saved my family life."

Roger closed his office door.

"What idea is that?" Ogden said. Bewildered, he looked around the room before his eyes settled on a Picasso lithocut of three nude women. He thought the lusty curves of the abstracted trio fit well with Roger's appetites.

"That business about the hobo," Roger said, still standing. "What other idea would I be talking about?" He asked Ogden to sit, and Ogden lowered himself into the familiar plushness of the brown velvet chair.

"Did you and the family find someone to play the Old MacDonald game?" Ogden said. One window in Roger's corner office faced directly toward the sea, and Ogden sighted the cargo ship he had seen from his office. It looked completely black now as its silhouette approached the sunny horizon.

"Sorry, Ogden," Roger said. "We didn't bother with Old Macdonald. Biff and Billy think that's a game for sissies—no offence to Johnny. You know how it is. My kids are a little older than your boy. It makes a big difference."

"No offence taken," Ogden said. He thought Roger's kids were a couple of red-headed hooligans—but he bit his tongue nonetheless. "What did your man do then? Did he sing? I could picture a rough-hewn down-on-his-luck tenor serenading your freckled family with the familiar strains of When Irish Eyes Are Smiling."

Roger shook his head and rolled his eyes. "You really are a square, Ogden," he said. "My kids like action, not pussy-ass songs. So I took your idea and put my own spin on it. I thought to myself, how can I entertain my family and friends—without boring them to death? That's when it came to me. My brother-in-law, Pete, owns a vacant warehouse in the Bronx—and there are plenty of bums around there. We scoured the streets for a couple of hours, found six hobos willing to fight for five-hundred dollars a piece, put them in a van, and took them to the warehouse. There, we formed a ring out of old crates and corrugated industrial containers and set the bums in the middle. We offered a thousand-dollar bonus to the last man standing and let them go at it. You should have seen them fight. One by one they went down until this burly Injun and some Rasta-man squared off in the makeshift arena.

"It really was a thing of beauty. I should have invited you and the fam—but I don't think fights are your game. Anyway, we all took bets on who would win. We were hooting and hollering. There were about twenty of us altogether. Even the wives ate it up. They drank wine and champagne straight from the bottle and cheered louder and louder whenever one of those bums fell. Then, once we were down to the wire—with only the Injun and the Jamaican left—Pete's son, Jack—I think you met him once—takes a two-by-four from beneath one of our chairs, runs to the ring, and tosses it into the middle. Those Jamaicans are supposed to be quick bastards, but that Injun out-footed him. He grabbed the two-by-four, cocked back his arms like a slugger about to crank one out of the park, and let loose—caught that Rasta right in the kisser. The guy didn't even have a chance to duck. Next thing we saw was a flare of blood, spit, and teeth hurling through the air. Then the Jamaican—dreads and all—crumpled to the floor. The Injun raised the two-by-four above his head, pumped it toward the roof a few times, and listened to us roar. He really knew how to work the crowd."

"And you didn't feel any guilt?" Ogden said, his eyes wide open. "What about the poor souls who suffered that Native American's wrath? Surely you must have tended to them."

"Don't be a baby, Ogden," Roger said. "If it makes you feel better, one of my friends is a doc, and he took the pulse of that Jamaican. He said the guy would live—at least until cirrhosis or Hepatitis C takes care of him. But, to make sure he didn't die right there and then, we dragged him outside and propped him against a steel fence. I'm sure—whenever he woke up—he crawled to an emergency room or one of those free clinics and got patched up there."

"Well, as long as there was a doctor onsite to attend to the injured," Ogden said, "I guess you had yourself covered. Those games of violence just aren't my cup of tea, but I'm glad you and your family were able to profit from my suggestion."

"Profit—damn straight I profited," Roger said, shooting a toothy grin at Ogden. "I had money riding on that Injun. In fact, I profited in more ways than one. Later that night, Martha and I went at it like a couple of teenagers. She couldn't get enough. I guess that fighting got her all stirred up. And, the next day, the kids carried on and on about watching those hobos beat one another to a pulp—they loved it."

"Was that the big news, then?" Ogden said. "Or was there something else—something about the Shakti file perhaps?"

"The big news?" Roger said, looking up at the ceiling and scratching his head. "Oh, yeah. In all the excitement, I almost forgot to tell you. I was so pleased with the way your idea turned out that I called up the other owners of the firm Saturday morning and talked to them about making you an equity partner. They were all on board with the suggestion, especially after I told them about your creative efforts to put the city's bums back to work. In fact, the paperwork's being prepared right now. You'll just need to sign some documents later, and it'll be official. You're a made man now."

Ogden pinched himself—literally—and asked Roger if he had heard him correctly. When Roger said he had, Ogden grinned from ear-to-ear. It was the culmination of Ogden's career at the firm—everything he had striven for over the last decade. "Thank you, Roger," he said. He felt giddy. He and Roger rose from their chairs. Over the leather inlay of Roger's desk, the two men shook hands to seal the deal.

As Ogden walked out of Roger's office, Roger called to him. "One last thing," he said. "Now that the partners know about your entertainment initiative, I'll bet there'll be a lot more employed hobos soon. You're a regular Mother Theresa. They might erect a statue in your honor someday." He winked at Ogden and laughed.

Ogden, still smiling, barely felt his feet touch the floor as he walked out of Roger's office.

THE FOLLOWING DAY, Ogden sat in his office and examined the Shakti file. Still giddy from yesterday's conversation with Roger, he struggled to analyze the pie charts, bar graphs, and other statistics from the company's most recent annual report. The numbers on the pages seemed to bleed into one another, and he could make neither heads nor tails of them. He struck his fist into his open hand, closed the annual report, and returned it to the file. After placing the file in his top right-hand drawer, he leaned back and rested the base of his head in the palms of his hands. He squeezed his interlocked fingers together and closed his eyes. The Shakti file can wait, he thought. In the meantime, I must determine how Sarah and

I can celebrate appropriately our recent good fortune. Since Johnny would be at a sleepover Friday night, he considered taking Sarah to dinner at a fine Italian restaurant. He mulled over the option for a while, but it smacked of mundanity in light of this week's extraordinary success. Moreover, when he thought of Sarah, he recalled their last two Friday evenings together and her late-night attempts to satisfy her passions with him. With good reason, he grew concerned about his inability to perform his manly duties. I must efface my deficiencies with her, he thought. But how can I assert my brutish lusts?

In response to this seemingly rhetorical question, Ogden's subconscious groped to replay his recurring dream of Hector and Consuela. He felt an immediate stirring in his loins. "Oh, Consuela," he muttered, picturing her ample buttocks vibrating in tiny waves—waves initiated by the brawny gardener's eager thrusts. Her cries of "Dios mio" echoed in his mind, and he licked his lips and surrendered to his naughty daydreams. Once again, he heard the groans and grunts of the bawdy pair as clearly as if he were kneeling beneath the windowsill of his family's servant's quarters. Rubbing his pee-pee instinctively, he lingered on the fantasy. Then—with a harsh staccato burst—his office phone rang. He shook his head and gathered his senses, quickly withdrawing his hand from between his legs. "Not at work!" he told himself. He sat upright in his chair, listened to the shrill rings, and allowed the incoming call to roll to voicemail.

Ogden's remembrance of his dream jogged his memory. He recalled that, several nights ago, he had envisioned a potential cure for his impotence. Still, the cure would necessitate sufficient scheming on his part to execute the desired outcome. Until now, he had felt thoroughly comfortable purchasing the services of riffraff to perform for him and his family. The desperate downtrodden needed money and were amenable to most requests. For this new plan to work, however, he would need to convince a colleague to play a very specific role. He knew that a man earning a six-figure income might be less eager to perform for Sarah and him. More than that, this colleague would need to maintain the utmost secrecy regarding their arrangement. Ogden—for one—would not want word of his escapades getting around the firm.

With that in mind, Ogden reasoned that ambition could often seal one's lips and trump one's need for money—and the young man whom he wished to employ had ambition in spades. Now, too, with his recent promotion, he had greater leverage to hoist the young man toward the next rung of his career ladder. In addition, the young man embodied to a T the role Ogden wanted him to play. After dissecting the pros and cons of his contemplated transaction, he determined the reward was worth the risk and took his first step to pursue the negotiation. He picked up his office phone and dialed. At the other end, a deep voice answered.

"Hello," Ogden said. "Am I speaking with Juan?...Please, call me Ogden...Why thank you, Juan. I'm quite honored that the firm would entrust me with such responsibility—I guess good news travels fast...By the way, would you please come to my office for a few minutes? I have a proposition I would like to discuss with you."

AT THE DOORWAY TO OGDEN'S office, Juan poked his head inside. "Good morning, Mr. Goodman," he said. He lowered his eyes and waited.

Ogden rose from behind his desk and approached the young man. "Come in—come in," he said. "And again, call me Ogden. No need to stand on ceremony with me." Juan stepped from the wood floor of the hallway onto the plush brown carpeting in Ogden's office. Ogden closed the door behind him. "Let's have a seat," he said. Draping an arm across Juan's shoulders, he led the strapping junior partner to the seat in front of his desk. Juan sat down. After resuming his place behind his desk, Ogden rested his elbows on its top and examined Juan closely. This sturdy hombre will surely fulfill my expectations, he thought.

Juan fumbled with his hands in his lap, and his eyes gazed downward.

As one who found no shame in appreciating a handsome man's features, Ogden admired Juan's assets. He noted the young man's full head of black hair, dimpled chin, and broad chest. Yes, he will surely do, he thought. If I dare say so myself, I think Sarah will find this young buck quite fetching.

"You said you wished to discuss something with me, Mr. Goodman—I mean Ogden," Juan said. He met Ogden's eyes briefly but continued to fumble with his hands.

"Yes, I do," Ogden said, "but we'll have time for that presently. Perhaps, at first, we can get to know each other a little better. If I recall correctly, you enjoy gazing at the skyline of this magnificent city. Am I right?"

"Very much so," Juan said. He looked over Ogden's shoulder toward the city's sun-soaked towers. "You may not know this, but my parents came to this country with almost nothing. They worked every day of my childhood to make sure I had the opportunity to go to a good school and succeed. Sometimes, after work, late at night, I walk across the Brooklyn Bridge just so I can walk back and see the spires of Manhattan illuminated beneath the clouds. When I bask in the glow of those lights and think of all of the millions of souls there struggling to succeed, I realize how much my family and I owe to this city and this country."

"Well spoken, Juan," Ogden said. "I could scarcely have expressed the essence of the American Dream in more concrete terms. Here, one can rise from a modest background, such as a cobbler or a bricklayer, to the highest pinnacles of success. More close to home for you, perchance, a child of immigrant parents can work night and day throughout his young adulthood to become a senior partner in a top law firm by the age of thirty. Would you not agree?"

"That is my desire Mr. Good—Ogden, I mean," Juan said. "I wish someday to make senior partner, but I am twenty-nine now and would gladly wait another couple of years to reach my goal."

"Don't sell yourself short, my young man," Ogden said. "There's an old adage that says, 'Much is given to whom much is expected'—or something to that effect. And, if I have my way, much will be given to you very, very soon. With my recent good fortune, my recommendations regarding career advancements will carry even more weight than they did before."

The olive complexion of Juan's cheeks grew rosy with the good news, and he smiled. "Thank you, Ogden," he said. "But what have I done to earn this great favor from you?"

Ogden returned Juan's smile and winked. "You haven't quite earned it yet," he said. "But you're very close—as I said before, from you 'much is expected.' Now, would you be willing to listen to a brief proposition I have for you?"

"Certainly, I would," Juan said, placing his hands on Ogden's desk. "It is an aspiration of mine to make senior partner in this firm. It would make my parents very proud. I would do whatever it takes."

Ogden looked at Juan's hands. He had long, thick fingers. You know what they say about big hands, Ogden thought. He raised his eyes to meet Juan's. "Hmmm—whatever it takes?" he said. "I like your initiative, young man. I'm assuming you would not be averse to mixing business with pleasure. Would you?"

"No, not at all," Juan said.

"Well, let me give you a better idea," Ogden said, leaning forward. Juan, too, bent toward Ogden until their heads nearly touched. Ogden could feel Juan's breath on his neck as he whispered into Juan's ear. "I would like to have a little get together this Friday night and would appreciate your presence..."

THAT FRIDAY NIGHT OGDEN arrived home early. He asked Maria to prepare dinner and set the table while Sarah was dropping Johnny off at a brownstone across town. Once Maria had finished, he thanked her, told her she could leave, and kissed her on the cheek before saying goodbye.

"Enjoy your night with the missus," Maria said, nodding to signal farewell.

Ogden closed the door behind her, straightened his tie, and returned to the dining area. Charles followed at his heels as Ogden walked through the condominium. He lit the three-light pewter candelabra that stood in the center of the table. After that, he went into the kitchen and turned on the oven to warm the food. Within seconds, Charles tilted his head, lifted one of his ears, and raced from the kitchen toward the front door. Standing by the stove, Ogden heard a key jostling in a lock.

"Honey, I'm home," Sarah said, opening the front door.

Ogden left the kitchen to greet his spouse. "Welcome back, my dear," he said. He paused in the television area, admiring Sarah's form-fitting sleeveless red summer dress. The dress accentuated her round hips and exposed her well-toned arms.

Sarah observed Ogden's interest and posed with one hand at her side and the other on the back of her head. She batted her eyelashes over her big blue eyes. "Like it," she said. "I bought it last week at Saks. It was on sale." She twirled around to give Ogden a full view.

"Hubba hubba," Ogden said. "You look ravishing this evening." He approached her, rested his arms on the small of her back, and kissed her.

"You can help me take it off later, if you'd like," Sarah said, winking at Ogden. "And ravishing of any sort would be appreciated."

Ogden playfully slapped Sarah's behind. "Someone is feeling a bit naughty tonight," he said. "She might even need a spanking later. But first, we should eat." He bowed low, holding his tie close to his chest. His upper body, poised parallel to the floor, pointed in the direction of the dining area. "Lady, your table awaits."

Sarah walked to the table, where Ogden helped her into her chair. In the kitchen, he served them each a broiled chicken breast, a large spoonful of green-bean casserole, and buttered corn-on-the-cob. He brought the plates over and sat at the head of the table, next to Sarah. She giggled after he finished saying grace. "I'm very excited about tonight," she said. "It's rare that we get an evening alone together."

Ogden, who had started to eat, set his chicken breast back on his plate. He cleared his throat. "We will be alone for the majority of the night," he said, dabbing the sides of his mouth with a white-linen napkin. "But I have procured a little entertainment first. A young man and woman will perform for us in a short time. It will be quite arousing. I assure you."

Sarah sighed. She set her hands in her lap. "I thought it would be just us," she said, shaking her head. "I was looking forward to some time alone with you."

Ogden took her hand in his, pressing it gently. "The entertainment will merely provide a precursor to an evening of erotic delights," he said. "I know I have not fulfilled my husbandly duties recently—and it pains me thoroughly. I want to make amends." He leaned toward her and kissed her on her cheek.

Sarah retreated from Ogden's show of affection. "But why do we need anyone else here tonight?" she said. She looked hard into Ogden's eyes.

Ogden whispered in her ear.

"They're going to do what?" Sarah said, sitting erect and pulling farther away from Ogden.

"Just you wait, darling," Ogden said. "Soon enough, every couple who can afford it will be following our lead."

JUAN ARRIVED FIRST. He wore soiled jeans and a stained white T-shirt. Ogden greeted him at the door. "Thank you for dressing according to my specifications," Ogden said. "That outfit sprouts fond memories in my fertile imagination."

Sarah, who had been pacing back and forth in front of the recently defunct television, dragged her red pumps across the wood floor as she approached Juan. Before she took his hand in hers, she looked at him quizzically, as if she were trying to place where she had met him before.

"Enchanted to see you again," Juan said, shaking Sarah's hand. He turned to Ogden. "Your wife looks even more stunning than she did at the Memorial Day party."

Sarah blushed. Her shoulders tensed with Juan's touch. "Why—you have some grip there," she said.

"And quite large hands," Ogden said, slapping Juan on the back.

Charles, having found a new playmate, hopped at Juan's feet and tapped his front paws on the guest's knees. Juan kneeled to pet him. "By the way, when will the lady arrive?" Juan said. "I'm eager to meet her."

"She should arrive any minute now," Ogden said. "And don't worry, Juan. I remember Roger mentioning this woman's employer a few weeks ago." He rolled his eyes. "That Roger—always into mischief with the ladies. He told me during one of our recent lunches that the company that employs this young vixen provides the best product in the city—ample women who keep themselves clean as a whistle." He put his arm around Sarah. "But I wouldn't know that from experience. I've got all I can handle right here."

Sarah relaxed slightly with Ogden's hug. She closed her eyes and rotated her head until her neck cracked. Ogden caressed one of her bare arms. The buzzer beside the front door rang. "I think your friend may have arrived," Ogden said to Juan. Ogden left Sarah's side, picked up the receiver, and spoke. "Yes, I am expecting another guest...a woman named Allegra...Yes, she's the one...Please, send her up." He returned the receiver to its place and rubbed his hands together. "This should be most delightful."

A few minutes later, a knock came at the door. At the sound, Charles whirled around the room and ran upstairs, nearly tripping Ogden along the way. Once Ogden recovered his balance, he opened the door. A young woman of average height with a large bosom and plump hips stood before him. She wore blue jeans and a white button-up blouse and held a small suit bag over her right arm. Her skin glowed the color of toffee under the bright lights. A thick crown of shoulder-length black hair framed her dark eyes, high cheekbones, and full lips. Ogden felt a twinge in his pants as he welcomed her to his home.

"Pase, por favor," Ogden said.

"Muchas gracias," Allegra said. She looked into the television area. "¡Ay, caramba! Quite a little party you have going on here. Now, will I be entertaining you or your friend? Or will we do switchies?" Allegra grinned at Sarah, whose face turned bright red.

"No, no, no," Ogden said. "Neither I nor my wife will be engaging in carnal pleasures with you or my friend." Sarah stared at her feet. Continuing to address Allegra, Ogden nestled against Sarah and took her hand in his. "Now, I see you brought a change of clothes with you, as I requested. Would you mind donning your costume? If you follow the wall to your left, it leads to the restroom. You are welcome to change in there."

Allegra followed Ogden's suggestion, and Ogden whispered in Sarah's ear. "Please, don't worry darling. After Juan and Allegra entertain us, we'll have the remainder of the evening to make naughty."

Sarah gripped Ogden's hand. "I'm just a little nervous," she said. "I've never watched two people do what they're about to do." She pursed her lips and squeezed her eyelids shut. "Well, I guess I did walk in on my parents once when I was a little girl—but I didn't watch."

"Why, darling, you grew up in a country home with a stable full of horses," Ogden said. "You must have seen a stallion mount a mare at some point. This will be quite a similar occurrence." Ogden turned to Juan, who stood a few paces away. He raised his voice to make certain Juan could hear. "Although this time the stallion will be named Juan. Right, my friend?"

Juan nodded. "Of course, Ogden," he said, crossing his arms at his chest. Damp rings of perspiration were visible beneath his armpits. His forehead glistened. He tapped his right foot on the wood floor.

Ogden noticed Juan's nervousness and sidled up to him. He put his arm around Juan's shoulders. "Everything will be all right, senior partner," he said, "or should I call you señor partner for this little dalliance." He patted Juan roughly on the back. "Remember, this is your chance to shine—Sarah and I eagerly await the coming performance of 'The Concupiscent Maid and the Ribald Gardener.'"

As if on cue, Allegra appeared from the hallway in a short black maid's outfit with lace fringe on the skirt and shirtsleeves. Strung tight like a corset, a white apron covered her midsection. Curtsying low, Allegra proffered Ogden and Juan a direct view of the upper lobes of her robust bosom. Ogden believed he could see the tops of her areolae radiating from the fabric. "¿Les gusta?" she said.

"Me gusta muchísimo," Juan said to Allegra. He cracked a smile and nudged Ogden. "Have no worries, Ogden. After catching a gander of this lusty lass, I'll have no trouble making this a cumming performance."

Ogden rubbed his palms together. "Now that's the spirit, my friend!" he said. He shot a glance at Sarah, who shuffled her feet and stared vacantly ahead. He hurried to her side. "Sarah, please, let's make our guests feel at ease. Have a seat on the sofa, and I'll dim the lights."

As Ogden darkened the room, Sarah took her place on the sofa. Hunching her shoulders, she crisscrossed her legs and pulled her arms close to her chest. Goosebumps appeared on her exposed skin, and her body trembled.

Ogden carried one of the chairs from the dining area and set it in front of the television. He leaned two pillows from the sofa against the legs of the chair. After setting the stage for the performance, he kneeled in front of the entertainment center and searched in his MP3 for appropriate music. He bypassed Stan Getz and Marvin Gaye, thinking them cliché for the atmosphere he wished to set. Yet, when he found Grover Washington Jr.'s album, Mr. Magic, he knew he had it. He struck the 'play' button with a flourish. Immediately, the smooth sounds of electric piano and bird tweets emanated throughout the room.

Juan moseyed over to Allegra, put his arm around her waist, and waited for the action to begin. "Wow!" Allegra said, admiring the way the limpid music seemed to seep from the walls. "This is some classy stuff. No Daddy Yankee here."

Allegra's accent, more Dominican than Mexican, grated on Ogden's ears, but he decided it must do for tonight. How different can "Dios Mio" sound in Dominican than it sounds in Mexican? he thought.

Raising his arms in the air to draw the attention of his guests, Ogden rose and provided the background for the upcoming performance. "Let's get started," he said, clapping his hands. "For this little vignette, Juan will play Hector the gardener, and Allegra will play Consuela the maid. Hector has just been working all morning in the hot sun. His hands are tired, but his libido is at its peak. Consuela, confined to her servant's quarters, yearns for this muscular man's passionate embrace. She invites him inside for an ice-cooled glass of lemonade. Still, the sweet liquid cannot douse the sparks that are soon to fly—now you two take it from here!"

Ogden struck his fist into the palm of his hand to signal the start of the action, then joined his wife on the sofa. "I think we are in for a humdinger of a show!" he said to Sarah. Sarah, her shoulders stooped, leaned forward.

Leading Juan into the center of the television area, Allegra paused by the black high-back chair. "Hector, are you still thirsty after planting all of those flowers in the garden?" Allegra said. "I could get you more lemonade if you desire."

"No, Consuela," Juan said. "That glass of lemonade quenched my thirst. But there is one thing it did not quench—my desire for you!"

"Oh señor," Allegra said, "I watched how lovingly you tended the shrubbery outside. But I fear you neglected something in your travails—you missed a bush."

"I would gladly tend to your bush, señorita," Juan said, "but I hope I have the right tool at hand."

"I think you have the necessary tool," Allegra said, facing Juan and groping his crotch. "And I do believe it is at hand." Juan grunted as she squeezed firmly.

To the whirling melody of a soprano sax, she unbuttoned Juan's jeans and pulled them and his underwear beneath his crotch. His thick, uncircumcised penis stood at half-mast. Dropping slowly to her knees, she stroked his shaft until she and Juan's member were head-to-head. "¡Ay papi!" she exclaimed, slipping a condom onto the gargantuan dong before taking Juan's girth into her mouth. As she fellated him, his member grew fully erect. In response, he groaned, letting his eyes roll toward the back of his head.

Sarah and Ogden observed from the couch. With her mouth agape, Sarah drew closer to the action. "Now I truly know what they mean when they say someone is hung like a horse," she said, her eyes bulging. "He reminds me of a chestnut Saddlebred my dad once owned. Do you think he's part African-American?"

Ogden rubbed her shoulders to loosen some of her tension. Her neck relaxed. "Don't go getting any ideas, my little butterfly," he said. "He's only for show."

Sarah slapped Ogden's thigh gently. "I didn't mean it like that," she said. "It would probably hurt anyway."

Ogden and Sarah huddled close together, entranced by Allegra's oral aptitude. Allegra swirled her tongue over Juan's glans, deep-throated the bulk of his organ, and bobbed her head back and forth like a chicken. Accompanying Allegra's deft movements, loud slurping sounds occasionally overpowered the sporadic surge of synthesizers. Amidst this bawdy cacophony, Juan added a constant chorus of ohhhs and ahhhs, his head lolling from side to side.

Without prompting, Ogden murmured to himself, "Oh, Consuela, you're a naughty, naughty nanny."

After about ten minutes, Allegra removed Juan's penis from her mouth. She formed a wide circle with her lips and rotated her jaw. "İQue grande!," she said. "I need to give my mouth a rest."

Juan pulled Allegra up from the floor and slapped her behind. "No rest for the wicked," he said as he guided her to the chair beside them. Throwing a pillow beneath her knees for comfort, he bent her over the chair, flipped her skirt above her waist, and pulled her panties to her knees. Her pink labia glistened with moisture. Letting his jeans fall to his ankles, he placed the other pillow on the ground and lowered himself behind Allegra. His sturdy biceps flexed as he steadied his swollen organ near Allegra's honeypot. She looked over her shoulder at him and moaned while he guided himself inside her.

"Oh my God!" Sarah said, her jaw dropping. "It barely fits." She gripped Ogden's thigh. Ogden put his hand on hers.

After the initial penetration caused Allegra's torso to stiffen, she wiggled her hips to accommodate the immense intruder. Juan allowed her to ease onto the full length of his shaft. His scrotum swayed lazily, occasionally slapping softly against Allegra's thighs.

"Me gusta mucho," Juan said. "Me gusta muchisimo."

Ogden goaded Juan's character to assert himself. "Hector," he said, "show her you mean business! Make her shout for the pleasure she seeks!"

Sarah gave Ogden a sidelong glance and saw his gaze affixed to Allegra's ample buttocks.

Following each of Juan's successive strokes, the flesh on Allegra's rear rippled. Ogden smiled and nodded. "That's the picture!"

Sarah guided her hand into Ogden's lap and found his penis hard as a rock beneath the fabric of his charcoal-gray trousers. Without looking away from the action, Ogden brushed her hand from his groin. "Not now, darling," he said. "Please wait until the performance is over. Isn't this marvelous?" He quickly looked at Sarah and saw that she had hiked her dress to the point where her panties nearly showed. Her fingers lingered tentatively on her inner thigh and made rapid, tiny circles on her skin.

"Gosh, he's really giving it to her now," Sarah said, focusing her stare on the action in front of them.

By now, the smooth funk of the album's third track had kicked in, and Juan rocked Allegra in rhythm to the sounds of a sultry saxophone and driving bass. A slight smell of perspiration and vaginal fluids permeated the television area. Mr. Magic had never sounded better, Ogden thought.

After a few minutes, the grunts, groans, and snorts of the carnally engaged couple grew more animated. Allegra, who likely had entertained a wide variety of men before, still seemed unaccustomed to the size of Juan's penis.

"My God!" she shouted repeatedly in response to Juan's deeper strokes.

"No, no, no!" Ogden shouted, a little disappointed. "¡Habla español, Consuela!"

Allegra, eager to please her customer, responded. "¡Dios mio!" she screamed. "¡Dios mio!"

Clapping, Ogden rocked back and forth on the sofa.

Unable to contain his pleasure and excitement, Juan's emotings grew louder and louder. "Ohohohohohoh!" he groaned, holding tightly to Allegra's hips. His head flopped in various directions, and his eyes glazed over. "İMe corro!" he shouted, pumping into Allegra more furiously. "İMe corro!" He drove three steady thrusts deep into Allegra, pushed out his chest, and loosed a long "Ohhhhhhhhhhhhhhhh!" After unloading his semen, he collapsed onto Allegra's back. Sweaty and half-clothed, the two performers rested, draped across the chair. They panted in unison.

"Good show!" Ogden said. "Bravo!" Applauding vigorously, he and Sarah stood in prolonged ovation.

"What a talented young man that Juan is!" Sarah said, smoothing her skirt so it once again covered her thighs. "And that Allegra was definitely convincing as a naughty maid."

"Which reminds me," Ogden said, winking his eye at Sarah, "we have some unfinished business to attend to." He took Sarah's hand and led her toward the stairs. Before mounting the first step, he turned back toward the sated and exhausted couple. "Juan, please see that that young lady gets home safely. Her negotiated fee—with a tidy bonus—is on the kitchen counter. You two were amazing—absolutely amazing!"

Without further ado, Ogden squeezed Sarah's rear and hurried her up the stairs.

Sarah glanced over her shoulder on the way to the bedroom and seemed surprised that she did not turn to salt. As her gaze lingered on the remnants of the orgiastic display below, "Black Frost," the final song on the album, faded to silence.

OGDEN AND SARAH RUSHED into their bedroom. It was dark, and Charles lay in the corner on his plush bed, his paws sheltering his eyes. Despite the commotion, Charles remained still and quiet. A dim light from the streetlamps below cast a yellow glow on one side of the bed. Sarah, her inner thighs wet from excitement, raced to the bed, and Ogden followed close behind. As Sarah attempted to hurl herself onto the mattress, Ogden enmeshed her in his arms.

"You won't escape that easily, my little butterfly," Ogden said. "I have scooped you into my net." He pressed her against the foot of the bed, doubled her over, and flipped up her skirt. Holding her down with one hand, he loosened his belt with the other. He dropped his trousers and underwear to the floor. "Now that I have you in my grasp, you will feel my sting!"

Beneath Ogden's strong clutch, Sarah squealed with delight. "Unhand me, you dirty, dirty beast!" she shouted, giggling and struggling to escape.

"I'll unhand you," Ogden said, "as soon as Little Willie here has had his taste of honey." He yanked Sarah's panties halfway down her thighs, inserted himself, and pumped furiously.

The two gabbled uncontrollably.

"Yes, Oggie doggy," Sarah said. "Yes! Yes! Yes!"

Within a few minutes, Ogden felt himself about to erupt. "I hope Daddy doesn't find out about this," he said, moving Little Willie in and out of Sarah. "He'll be sure to punish us both if he does. Why does it feel so good to be so naughty???!!! Blaaaaaaaa!!!"

IN THE FOLLOWING WEEK, Ogden's good fortune continued. Roger and the two other equity partners invited him to move into the remaining corner office on their floor. The office had been vacant since a prior equity partner died six months ago, a few days before Christmas. A belated holiday gift, Ogden thought as he viewed Lady Liberty from this new, more prestigious vantage.

That week, too, Juan officially received his promotion.

Ogden personally lobbied the other equity partners to allow Juan to occupy Ogden's former office. "I believe the young man deserves it," Ogden told them. "Besides, it will look good for clients of our firm to see some color in one of our premier offices. Right now, the few darker faces seem relegated to the galleys below. To quote a modern troubadour, my friends, 'the times they are a changin.'"

The partners harrumphed a bit, but eventually they agreed.

When Juan learned he would move into Ogden's old office, he tracked Ogden down in the hallway. "Ogden," he said, "I don't know how to thank you. I called my father and mother already. My parents have never been more proud."

"You have thanked me enough, señor partner," Ogden said, grinning widely. The two chuckled, and Ogden playfully punched Juan in the arm. "I must say, your performance was quite a big surprise to Sarah and me—with the emphasis on big." Ogden closed his eyes briefly and recalled Juan plowing into Allegra, her buttocks rippling. Once more, he felt a familiar twinge in his pants.

"Thank you again," Juan said, blushing.

"No need for additional thanks," Ogden said, holding out his hand. "Now give me that meaty paw of yours and let's speak no more on it."

The two men shook hands and never mentioned the matter again.

ON WEDNESDAY, OGDEN met Roger for lunch. Roger finished his first martini and ordered another. His eyes bleary, he nodded toward a buxom redhead who sat at the table beside them. "A couple of weeks ago, I would have risked the rack to put my johnson between that rack," Roger said. "Now, thanks to you, I alleviate my stress and frustration in other ways. You know what the family and I did on Saturday night?"

"No," Ogden said. "Pray tell."

"We played a little game my sons called 'The Gauntlet.'" Roger said, chuckling. "Where those boys get this stuff I'll never know—must be the Internet. Anyway, we picked up eight migrants outside a Home Depot—offered them a thousand dollars each with a thousand-dollar bonus for the winner. We had them line up in a hallway at the vacant warehouse, and about twenty of us—even the wives—stood on either side with two-by-fours in our hands. My friend Bill stood behind those bums with a baseball bat and prodded them forward. Whoever made it through still standing had to run the gauntlet again until there was no one left. Most of those guys crumpled the first time through, especially if they got clubbed in the stomach or the shins. As soon as they fell to the ground, my sons descended on them and finished them off. It was a hoot! Only two of those Josés made it through the first time, but one of them was dazed after being knocked in the head. He couldn't wobble more than a few yards the second time before being struck down like a cockroach. That other one was crafty, though. Quick as a whip—and limber too. I think we only glanced him with five or six blows each run. As soon as he made it through and realized he'd won, he collapsed on the floor and cried like a baby. We all hollered and raised hell. I tell you—it beats sitting in front of the boob tube on Saturday nights!"

Ogden shook his head in disapproval. "Roger, Roger," he said. "I can't understand why you delight in other people's misery." Still, he reasoned that these migrants had willingly accepted an offer for which they had been compensated. They had been free actors in the negotiation process. Perhaps the one-thousand dollars would go far to support their families in their home countries. He looked at his open hands, which rested palms-up on the table. "To each his own, I guess."

Roger downed his drink and coughed into a closed fist. Raising his empty glass, he toasted. "To the winners—and the losers," he said.

"Yes," Ogden said. "May we always be counted among the former." He touched his glass of soda water to Roger's glass. "By the way, Roger, I believe I'll take the next two days off—as vacation. The Fourth falls on Sunday this year, and I would like to plan a little get together. Would that be all right?"

Roger placed his glass on the table and shrugged his shoulders. "You're an owner in the firm now," he said. "You make your own hours. As long as our clients are happy—and the money's coming in—do as you please."

Ogden tipped his head. "Very well then," he said. "I would like you and your family to join us for this holiday soiree—and I'll invite our new senior partner, Juan, as well. We've developed a unique mentor-mentee relationship recently."

"We'll be there," Roger said. "What do you have planned for this little shindig?"

Rubbing his hands together, Ogden smiled. "You'll have to wait and see."

OGDEN SPENT THE FOLLOWING three days preparing for his Fourth of July party. To gather his "recruits," he visited a soup kitchen in Chelsea at lunchtime on Thursday. As a group of smelly, bedraggled individuals queued outside an iron gate beneath the shadow of a tall black spire, he walked the line offering bounties to individuals who would fill the ranks of his ragtag corps. He promised nine-hundred dollars—three-hundred dollars per day—to each man who would commit to three-days work. "It will be hard work, not for the faint-hearted," he harangued, staring the hungry men in the eyes. "You will get one-hundred dollars if you report to me at eleven-hundred hours at Grant's Tomb in Riverside Park. You will receive the remainder of your bounty upon completion of your task on Sunday afternoon. Now let me have a show of hands of those interested."

About fifty men raised their hands.

That makes half a company, Ogden thought. It will have to do, I guess. He ordered the men to report tomorrow sharply at the aforementioned time and location and to appear there showered and clean shaven.

The men who volunteered studied their captain with amusement, smiling at the man who stood before them in a tailored linen suit with his hazel eyes burning beneath the noontime sun.

Before leaving, Ogden asked these men to step forward and, after they did, he shook the hands of his recruits. He thanked them for their courage and told them that the satisfaction they would get from their service would make up for the labor they would expend.

"Just don't work us too hard, Guv'nor," one of the men said, giggling and nudging in the ribs the man standing next to him.

His jaw clenched, Ogden glowered at the fellow. "That's 'captain' to you, my friend," he said, stepping close to the man. "And you would best be served to show more respect to your commanding officer."

Trembling, the man avoided Ogden's eyes by staring at his furrowed brow. He realized that Ogden was not joking. "Yes, sir, captain, sir!" the man shouted, puffing out his chest and saluting.

Ogden nodded his head in approval. "Much better, soldier," he said. "At ease." He stepped back and surveyed the line. "Tomorrow. Eleven-hundred hours. Sharp!" He turned, strode down the sidewalk, and left the men to continue waiting in line for their meals.

AT HOME, OGDEN ORDERED online—with overnight delivery—forty union-soldier uniforms in various sizes and forty wooden rifles. He assumed a twenty- to thirty-percent attrition rate from the fifty volunteers he had recruited. Among other things, this assumption accounted for the losses of no-shows, the infirm, and drunkards. I'll be surprised if at least ten men don't drop from tomorrow's training alone, he thought. He reasoned he could return the surplus uniforms and recoup a portion of his outlay if necessary. Money, however, was no object, and he eagerly planned for the amusement of his guests.

After ordering the necessities for his recruits, Ogden called his household into the television area. Sarah, Johnny, and Maria gathered around him. As usual, Charles milled about their feet. Ogden explained that they would have a little holiday cheer at their home on Sunday and asked Maria if she would be willing to work that day.

"Of course," Maria said. "Anything for el jefe."

Ogden hitched his thumbs in his pockets and stood ramrod straight. "Soon," he said, "el jefe will become el capitan!" He handed Maria a list. "Maria, please purchase these things to stock our larder. I think a feast of traditional American fare will satisfy our Independence-Day appetites."

"Certainly, Mr. Goodman," Maria said. "I will run to the store this afternoon."

Sarah pulled Ogden aside. "Who exactly will be coming?" she said, staring at her feet.

"Roger and his family," Ogden said. "And Juan, perhaps, with a guest."

"Juan will be here?" Sarah said. She blushed.

Ogden put his arm around her. "Now, now, now, my little butterfly," he said. "Juan and I have an understanding. We agreed to speak no more about our voyeuristic episode the other night. It's as if it never happened."

"All right," Sarah said. "I'll do my best not to think about it. It just might be hard, especially if we're eating frankfurters."

THE FOLLOWING DAY, a little before eleven-hundred hours, Ogden paced beside the granite and marble mausoleum that housed the remains of the man he considered to be the greatest general in US history. Arcing his neck to view the white dome that glimmered beneath the summer sun, he whispered, "Oh great general, give me strength today. My task may not be fraught with as much peril as yours, but it is a noble task nonetheless—as is any task that strives to honor God and country." He bowed his head and prayed silently to himself. When he opened his eyes, he saw the first recruits emerge from a city bus. Soon, several more joined him on the plaza in front of the monument. As the recruits gathered before him, he counted forty-two men.

With a solid step, Ogden mounted the stairs leading to the mausoleum and stood on a platform flanked by two stone eagles. A small crowd of tourists and spectators gawked at the sight of a man in a crisp summer suit about to speak to a ragtag group of seemingly destitute individuals. Some of the tourists snapped photographs, but Ogden paid them no mind.

Clapping his hands to draw the attention of his volunteer army, Ogden addressed his soldiers. "You may not know this yet," he said, raising his arms to the heavens. "But two days from now, I expect you to make me very proud. Yet, as proud as I will be to see us achieve this stunning task, my pride will not match the dignity you will find in yourselves—the dignity that comes with hard work, noble sweat, and the ability to put food on your and your family's table. Now, don't be mistaken, I will drive you—and drive you hard—but, if you succeed, you will have nine-hundred dollars to your name—and something else much, much more valuable—the knowledge that there is life beyond the dole." He looked down upon the mass of nodding men, all of them clean shaven and recently scrubbed.

"Are you all in?" Ogden shouted.

"Yes, sir!" they responded in unison.

"I can't hear you!" Ogden cried, cupping his hand to his ear.

"Yes, sir, captain, sir!" the men shouted.

His head held high, Ogden descended the stairs into the midst of his saluting citizen soldiers. He reached into his pocket and pulled out a wad of one-hundred dollar bills. He distributed his initial payment to his men. "Eight-hundred more awaits each man who sees this through to the end," he said.

After Ogden had finished handing out the bills, a slovenly man ran across the plaza toward him. The man arrived, unkempt and unshaven, and stood panting before Ogden.

"Private Jackson here reporting for duty," the man said, standing at attention. Ogden recognized the man as the miscreant who had called him "Guv'nor" the previous day.

The man held out his hand for his expected payment.

Ogden cocked his head and squinted his left eye. "Jackson, eh," he said. Shaking his head, he looked at his watch. "You're ten minutes late, Jackson."

"I lost track of time, Captain," Jackson said, tittering. "I was busy with my girlfriend—if you know what I mean."

Ogden chuckled. "Aaaah," he said. "I'll give you something truly to get busy about. You better get busy and lose that smirk, young man. Now skedaddle!"

With a dismissive flip of his wrist, Ogden turned from Jackson toward his troops. "Let this be a lesson to you all. I will not tolerate tardiness or insubordination of any sort—such behavior will result in your immediate dismissal and a forfeiture of your final payment. Do you understand?"

"Yes, sir, captain, sir!" the throng bellowed in unison.

Defeated and humiliated, Private Jackson bowed his head and shuffled across the plaza whence he came.

FOR THE REMAINDER OF the day, Ogden instructed his troops in basic marching maneuvers. Beneath the July sun, the men sweated, their perspiring bodies filling the air with a fetid odor. The passersby, initially intrigued, eventually dispersed, presumably believing that Ogden and his soldiers were merely part of a civil-war reenactment unit.

After several hours of drill, a soldier fell to the ground, exhausted from the heat and exercise. Others fell soon after.

Ogden furloughed those men, with a day's pay, and instructed them not to return. He wished to maintain a strong company, absent of any weak links. As evening fell, nine men had succumbed to exhaustion or heat stroke.

The following day, Ogden dispersed the uniforms and rifles to his remaining thirty-three soldiers. He nicknamed them "the fighting 107th," after a monument in the park near where he and his family lived.

Of the men, one soldier in particular, a young man named Josh Chamberlain, had excelled in all manner of drills. Ogden appointed Chamberlain to the position of sergeant, putting him in charge of the thirty-two corporals. Soon thereafter, he confided in Chamberlain his plans for the Fourth of July. Keeping a stern eye on his charges, Sergeant Chamberlain acknowledged Ogden's plans and nodded his assent.

Under Sergeant Chamberlain's command, the men continued to drill throughout the gloaming. Ogden watched them silently from beneath the lengthening shadow of the tomb. When the last light of the setting sun danced upon the Hudson River, Ogden gathered his forces together.

"I found you men two days ago outside a soup kitchen with hardly a penny to split amongst one another," Ogden said, pacing and holding his hands behind his back. "Now, after several long hours of hard work, you stand at the cusp of having nine-hundred dollars to each of your names. You should be proud. You may—many years from now—look back at these few days as the start of your journey on the road toward achieving the American Dream. I hope, with fondness, you will recall my role in your future successes. But, for now, we have other challenges close at hand. Tonight, my soldiers, rest well, and report to Sergeant Chamberlain in Central Park at fourteen-hundred hours tomorrow. If you perform as well then as you have the past two days, you will arouse my pleasure—and, perhaps, even earn a slight bonus. Are you with me, my friends?"

"We're with you, Captain Goodman—each and every one!" one of the men shouted.

A hearty "Hurrah!" rose from the mass of men and echoed within the stone hollows of Grant's Tomb.

ON THE MORNING OF THE Fourth, Ogden woke to distant bellows. He cast aside his blankets and hurried to the window. He chewed his fingernails as he watched the thunderous spectacle outside. Lightning flashed across the park, accompanied by claps that clattered like cymbals and booms that quaked the sky—but, within minutes, the storm clouds, black and undulating, moved swiftly southward, leaving sunlight and blue skies in their wake. He breathed a sigh of relief.

Sarah, rubbing the sleep from her eyes, yawned. "Is everything all right, darling?" she said. "It sounds like we had quite a storm."

Ogden glanced again through the curtains. "No need to worry, my little butterfly," he said. "The heavens often rend their garments at moments of portentous change. Then, once they have dutifully mourned the loss of the defeated age, they welcome the tranquility of the new order. I believe something similar occurred on the day of Lincoln's Second Inaugural."

Ogden turned from the window, letting the warmth of the sun fall upon the back of his neck. He began his preparations for the day. He shaved, showered, and dressed for the occasion, donning a freshly pressed white-linen suit, a light-blue dress shirt, and a dark-blue tie. In his lapel, he placed an American-flag pin.

When Ogden approached Sarah, who still lay in bed, she pulled him toward her by his tie. Whispering in his ear, she said, "Would you let me take that suit off of you for a few minutes, Oggie doggie? I'm feeling a little tingly in my naughty parts."

Ogden kissed her cheek but released himself from her grip. "Not now, Sarah," he said. "Today must go smoothly—with no complicating entanglements." He brushed the stray hairs away from her eager blue eyes. "But I promise you, we will celebrate later—perhaps this evening you can mount my flagpole as the night sky erupts with fireworks."

Sarah smiled and moved one of her hands beneath the crumpled top sheet. "OK," she said. "You promised—and don't think I won't forget." She giggled. "Now why don't you run off and do what you need to do. I think I'll stay here in bed and rest a while."

"Don't sleep too late, darling" Ogden said, withdrawing toward the bedroom door. "We have a busy day ahead!" On the way out, he donned a skimmer hat with a red, white, and blue band that circled his head.

THE GUESTS BEGAN ARRIVING shortly after one o'clock—to the musical accompaniment of John Philip Sousa's Stars and Stripes Forever. Roger arrived first with his two sons, Biff and Billy. Roger told Ogden that his wife Shannon was feeling ill and could not attend.

Wearing a blue hunting shirt, white breeches, and a black tricorn hat, Johnny ran haphazardly from his bedroom upstairs into the television area. Johnny circled Biff and Billy, jumping up and down. "Will you play Old MacDonald with me?" he said. Charles, who hid behind the corner of the sofa, poked his black-and-white head out to growl at Roger's two freckle-faced children, whose red hair blazed like the devil's skin.

"Billy will play with you," Biff said. "Right, Billy?" Biff tugged Billy's ear, and Billy slapped Biff's hand away.

"No I won't," Billy said. "That game's for sissies."

Cackling, Biff punched Billy in the stomach, and Billy doubled over.

"Dad!" Billy shouted, sniffling and wheezing.

Roger grabbed Biff by the hair and boxed his ears. "You two brats will do whatever Johnny wants," he said. "Johnny, start your Old MacDonald game. Biff can play a jackass, and Billy—that little coward—can play a chicken. Bock bock-bock Bock Bock bock-bock." Roger clucked and pecked like a chicken before kicking Billy in the seat of his pants. "Now scram, you creeps!"

As the children hustled upstairs, a knock came at the front door. Maria opened it. Juan and a buxom blonde walked in. Juan led his guest across the threshold, guiding her with his hand upon her rear. After removing his palm from his guest's behind, he turned to Maria. He took Maria's hand in his and kissed it.

"Hola, guapa," Juan said.

Maria blushed. "Mr. Goodman," she said, smiling. "A very charming guest is here to see you."

Ogden approached the couple and shook Juan's hand. "I see you brought Jennifer, the new intern," he said. "I'm glad the two of you could make it." Leaning close to Juan, he whispered, "Good choice, young man. Good choice."

Juan paused to scan the condominium. "This place looks much more festive than the last time I was here," he said. He remarked how much he liked the American-flag garlands that festooned the walls. "And where did you get that star-spangled bunting that's hanging beneath the kitchen window? ¡Que americano!"

As Maria took Juan aside and told him where she had purchased the decorations, Roger asked Ogden to join him in the kitchen. With a rivulet of drool escaping from the side of his mouth, Roger stared over his shoulder at Juan and his guest. "Lucky Mexican bastard," he said. "He's going to ream Suzy Sunshine over there with his pork enchilada." He sighed and shook his head. "And I thought she would spend this summer assisting me with my briefs—if you know what I mean."

As the two men walked past the dining area, Ogden noticed that Roger's hands were shaking. Moreover, he saw that his friend's eyes appeared bloodshot and unsteady.

"Is everything all right, Roger?" Ogden asked. "You seem a little out of sorts."

Roger approached the kitchen sink, leaned against it, and rested his head in his hands. His hands, which continued to shake, caused his gaunt cheeks to tremble. "I really need a stiff drink," he said. "I haven't had one yet." The smell of hot dogs and baked beans emanated from the stove to his right, and Roger clutched his stomach.

Ogden patted Roger on the back. "Rest assured that I can cure what ails you," he said. "I bought Hendrick's just for the occasion. I know it's your favorite." Ogden opened a cabinet beneath the sink, fished out the gin, dry vermouth, and cocktail olives, and set them on the counter. "I never touch the stuff myself, but I can mix a mighty delectable beverage—at least that's what I'm told."

After using a pewter cocktail shaker to blend the ingredients with ice, Ogden poured the clear concoction into a martini glass, added three olives, and handed it to Roger.

Roger guzzled half of the drink and refilled it with the dregs from the shaker. He hacked from the initial sting of the alcohol, but his hands steadied instantly. "Shannon left me last night," he said, massaging his temples. "Ran off with some amateur MMA fighter—at least that's what she called him. Some bum she met at the gym. I haven't told the kids yet. They actually believe she's sick."

"I'm sorry to hear that," Ogden said. He patted Roger on the back. "Perhaps she'll return before the children even notice. Women can be rash. I'm sure she'll come to her senses soon enough."

"It's more than that," Roger said, spitting into the sink. "I think she really is a little sick—in the head. It seems like all that violence from our parties really got her juices flowing." He closed his eyes and clenched his teeth. "Tell me, Ogden. How can I compete with some muscle-bound bonehead when it comes to violence? And get this—the guy's ten years her junior! And worse—he's black! A negro, Ogden! A negro!"

"Now, now, Roger," Ogden said. "I've often heard that Caucasians of both sexes experiment in such ways. I think the term for such an affliction is 'jungle fever.' I'm sure she'll recover from this disorder soon and return to you on bended knee."

"Ogden, I'm not so certain," Roger said. "Haven't you heard the phrase, 'Once you go black, you never go back?' It could be true."

Before they could finish their conversation, Sarah appeared in the entryway to the kitchen. Her cheeks flush, she wore a low-cut white sundress, red ruby earrings, and a turquoise necklace. She batted her eyelashes at Ogden. "I hope I'm not interrupting anything," she said.

"No, no, my darling," Ogden said. "We were just discussing the Shakti case." He put his hand on her shoulder, which felt clammy with sweat. "Are you OK? You look agitated."

"I'm all right," she said. Her cheeks shifted from pink to crimson. "Really—I haven't been doing anything unusual. I was just getting ready for the party. Sometimes it takes me a while."

Ogden cocked his head, squinted, and examined Sarah up and down. He wondered whether the morning's urges had defeated her self-control—but he decided to question her about that later. He cleared his throat. "Enough said," he commented.

"You're a lucky man, Ogden," Roger said, leering at the goose bumps on Sarah's arms and bosom. He patted Ogden strongly on the back. "A damn lucky man." Without another word, he turned back toward the sink and fixed himself another martini.

From outside the kitchen, Maria shouted. "Mr. Goodman, you said you wanted lunch at one thirty. I better get moving before it's too late!"

Ogden hurried Roger and Sarah from the kitchen. Roger's martini lapped over the rim of his glass and trickled to the floor as he scurried behind Sarah. His eyes seemed locked on the movement of Sarah's swaying hips.

Oh, that Roger! Ogden thought. Always thinking of fornication. What a dirty hound!

While the Goodmans and their guests mingled in the dining area, Maria dished out lunch for everyone. Each person received a hot dog and sides of baked beans, potato salad, and coleslaw—a traditional Independence-Day feast.

Once Maria had finished serving the adults, Ogden called the children down from upstairs to fetch their plates. After each person had a plate in hand, the celebrants gathered around the table to fix their hot dogs with a variety of condiments. The feasters chose from mustard, catsup, sauerkraut, green relish, chopped onions, and hot sauce.

Sarah watched Juan lather his frankfurter with relish. She huddled close to Ogden. "I really think Maria should have given him a foot-long," she said. "Don't you?"

Ogden provided all of the adult guests with Sam Adams beers. He handed cans of Coca-Cola to the children and opened a bottle of Saratoga mineral water for himself. Before anyone began eating, he took a fork from the table and tapped the neck of his bottle to gather everyone's attention.

"Here, here," Ogden said. He raised his hand to silence his guests. "I know you are justifiably famished, but—as proud and dutiful Americans—we should take a moment to reflect upon the importance of this hallowed day before we enjoy this delicious repast.

"As you are well aware, nearly two centuries and two-score years ago, our country's fathers stared unblinkingly into the fanged maw of their oppressor and signed a document some, at the time, called treasonous. That daring action—in conjunction with the blood shed by countless patriots—gave birth to this nation of which we are so proud. Yet, on another less-remembered Independence Day—one that occurred exactly one-and-a-half centuries ago this day—our nation, torn by racial and sectional strife, teetered on the brink of destruction. Still, that morning, blessed providence shone once again on this land. A bright July sun woke the supporters of the Union and heralded to them news of victory on the fields of Gettysburg. Moreover, later that same day, these self-same supporters raised their glasses to celebrate as twilight graced them with word of the surrender of Vicksburg, the Gibraltar of the West. They knew then that this Union would be preserved. Certainly, my friends, this is a hallowed day indeed.

"And now, where do we stand as Americans? Surely, the battles we wage in our day-to-day lives rarely end in bloodshed—but are they less important? Each day, when we walk outside, we encounter the scourges of poverty, illness, and indolence. Should we turn a blind eye to the disadvantaged masses? Or should we grant them the opportunity to pull themselves up by their bootstraps? I insist we do the latter—for a nation that could produce a Jefferson, a Washington, a Lincoln, and a Grant can indubitably produce men and women willing to work for an honest day's wage. Soon enough, my friends, you will see ample proof of this. Soon enough, indeed."

Ogden, his face red with excitement, reached into his jacket pocket to remove a starched white handkerchief. As his guests applauded his impromptu speech, he dabbed the sweat from his brow.

"Bravo," the guests shouted. "Bravo!"

Ogden glanced at his watch. It was nearly two o'clock.

Raising his bottle of water into the air, Ogden again pleaded for silence. With the wide eyes of his guests upon him, he uttered the final words of his toast: "Let us drink now to those who made this beloved country what it is today—and to those of us who will shape its future!"

The guests nodded in agreement.

"Amen!" slurred Roger, who set his empty glass on the table and hoisted his beer to his lips.

As everyone else began to eat, Ogden opened the window in the dining area as wide as possible. The sounds of the street below crept into the room. Car horns honked, sirens blazed, and crosswalk signals buzzed. Still, Ogden listened closely for other sounds, awaiting the distant murmur he expected to come momentarily.

Before Ogden could hear the sounds he anticipated, Charles' ears perked. Dodging the feet of the guests, the dog tilted its head and scrambled around the table. When it approached the window, it stood with its front paws upon the bunting and hopped up and down in an attempt to see over the windowsill.

Ogden looked across the street and saw in the distance four columns lined eight men deep. The men marched through the park, their feet stamping in solid time. With Sergeant Chamberlain leading them along the paved path, they slowly approached. The faux soldiers carried false wooden rifles in their right arms, the harmless barrels pointing toward the sky.

Spectators in the park gathered around the men, but the soldiers marched on, seemingly unimpressed by the attention.

Ogden strained to hear the soldiers' voices over the din outside, but could not. Johnny's young ears, however, were more capable.

Removing his hat from his head and running to the window, Johnny nudged against his father. He loomed over Charles, who continued to leap against the bunting.

"I hear my song," Johnny said. "Daddy, someone's singing my song!"

Ogden listened closer and closer. Soon, he recognized various sounds: the stomp of the soldiers' footsteps as their feet marked time against the pavement, the shouts of Sergeant Chamberlain at passersby as he ordered them to make way, and the clamor of his guests as they jostled to gather around the window. Then, like a choir of angels on the wind, the voices of thirty-two men singing as one wafted through the window:

"When Johnny comes marching home again,
Hurrah! Hurrah!
We'll give him a hearty welcome then
Hurrah! Hurrah!
The men will cheer and the boys will shout
The ladies they will all turn out
And we'll all feel gay when Johnny comes marching home..."

Sarah, Maria, and the guests stood on tiptoes and craned their necks to glimpse the company of men dressed in Union blue. Juan pushed forward and took his place beside Ogden. Roger squeezed in next to Juan and pressed his head against Juan's shoulder. From where he stood, Roger could barely see out the window.

Outside, flanked by the newly mown grass, the soldiers marched, a small sea of blue drifting along the black tar. Propelled by the steady beat of their marching feet, the men continued their song.

Clapping his hands, Johnny hopped up and down in front of Ogden. Ogden held Johnny's shoulders.

"What do you think of the show, Johnny?" Ogden said.

"This is the greatest Fourth of July ever!" Johnny shouted.

Ogden smiled. "Better than when Pemberton surrendered Vicksburg to Grant?" he said.

Johnny lifted his head and met his father's eyes. He took Ogden's hands in his. "Better," he said. "Much better."

Ogden spoke again, to himself this time, but loud enough that those around him could hear. "This world belongs to us and those like us—those duly blessed by providence," he said. "The rest are players on our stage. With the proper guidance—and the right incentives—they will gladly perform for us as soldiers, fools, or kings. We must only strike the proper bargain, and they'll be ours."

Ogden held Johnny close and tousled his son's white-blonde hair. Below him, the soldiers approached the sidewalk at the park entrance, halted, and stood at attention.

With his rifle angled across his chest, Sergeant Chamberlain barked his command. "Company, salute!" he said.

At that moment, the thirty-two men behind him raised their hands to their foreheads in honor of their absent captain.

Ogden imagined that the soldiers' eyes searched the windows in front of them for the sturdy silhouette of Captain Ogden Goodman. He imagined that they saw the upright shadows of him and his son—and, if they further strained their eyes, they saw the tall shadow of his new partner and the half-shadow of the drunken Roger.

Ogden, squinting from the bright sunlight, raised his arm and returned the salute of his troops. Briefly, he gazed over the treetops and contemplated the never-ending heavens.

Without a word, Ogden closed the window, drew the shades, and turned toward the table. The smiling faces of his family and guests settled upon him.

The world—and all it offered—was his.

Author's Bio:

Lewis J. Beilman III lives in Hamden, Connecticut, with his family, dog, and two cats. He writes fiction in his spare time. His stories have appeared in Foliate Oak Literary Magazine, ArLiJo, Reed Magazine, and other literary publications. In 2009, he won first prize in the Fred R. Shaw Poetry Contest.

Outside of writing, Lewis enjoys reading, playing soccer, and volunteering in his community. He has a law degree from the University of Maine Law School and a bachelor's degree in political science from Sacred Heart University—but he is first and foremost a writer.

You can find out more about Lewis at www.lewisbeilman.com and on Twitter and Instagram @LJBeilman3.

Blurbs:

"[Lewis] Beilman casts the satirist's stink eye on the gilded lives of the bored and wealthy. Fourth of July is a clever, absurdist tale for the Opposite World where we all dwell now."

Debra Dean, author of The Madonnas of Leningrad

"Grounded in scene and propelled forward by a satirically dark portrayal of white privilege, Fourth of July boldly depicts the bigotry, racism, and sheer absurdity that still plague contemporary American life. Refusing to offer easy answers or feel-good resolutions, this daring novella forces us to confront issues of class, race, and culture through a seemingly hyperbolic lens that at times can feel all too real. Anchored by self-assured prose, Lewis Beilman skillfully balances an incrementally disturbing plot and cast of central characters with a touch of humor, all of it leading to a powerfully unsettling conclusion. In today's social and political context, Fourth of July is sure to linger long after it has been read."

Dariel Suarez, author of In the Land of Tropical Martyrs

Acknowledgements

I would like to thank the following for their support in the creation of this novella: Jennifer Saunders, the love of my life, and our son, Je'nigh Ward, for their constant support; my best friend, Joseph Boski, for years of encouragement; Dariel Suarez, a great friend and author, for his valuable writing advice; Debra Dean and Dr. Michael Hettich, for mentoring me as an author; my mother, father, step-mother, brothers, in-laws, and extended family for reading much of my work, even the crappy stuff; my friend and fellow writer, Noah Messing, for lending me a writing space; my publisher, Roxana Nastase of Scarlet Leaf Publishing, for having faith in this story; and all of the others whom I may have missed but who helped me on my journey.